The time is a h[...] Danny Davidson co[...] [...]dogs to perform for the crowd at Galena, Illinois. From here he and his father plan to join a stage troupe playing before miners in the Colorado gold fields.

But Danny at fourteen finds himself traveling westward without his father. Soon he knows the thrill of hearing an audience applaud him and learns he must accept sudden sorrow.

Abby Mason and her family offer Danny friendship in the fast-growing, sometimes dangerous mining town of Central City. At Glorieta Pass, often called the "Gettysburg of the West," Danny meets hardship with courage.

Here's an adventure story that makes the ghost towns of Colorado live again. The background for the action is based on fact, and many of the characters are real people from pioneering days in the West.

Gold Dust and Bullets

UNDER THE
GASLIGHT
A THREE ACT PLAY

STARRING
THE
LANGRISHES

GOLD DUST

and

BULLETS

Florance Walton Taylor

★

Illustrated by

William Granstaff

★ ★ ★

Chicago, Illinois

ALBERT WHITMAN & COMPANY

E524516

j T2144 g0

To Betsy
with love

CONTENTS

PART ONE

HEADED WEST

★ ★ ★ ★ ★ ★ ★ ★ ★ ★

CHAPTER I

Step Right Up!

The tall, thin man set up a small table on Main Street. Then he tugged at a large satchel and lifted it slowly out of the one-horse cart. That cart had already come a long way, from New York to Illinois.

Turning to the boy beside him, the man asked, "All ready with the dogs and your harmonica, Danny?"

"All set," Danny Davidson answered and released two little white dogs, one a spitz and the other a poodle, from their leash. He put his harmonica to his lips and began a merry tune.

While the boy played, his father took out a few bottles of Duffy's Elixir from the satchel and set them on the table.

Step Right Up!

"Step right up, folks! See the wonderful dog show!" the tall man shouted to the passers-by. "See Missy and Tuffy do their amazing tricks! Missy and Tuffy, straight from New York!"

It was a hot morning that June day of 1861, but the streets of Galena were crowded with levee workers, lead miners, and women going to market. Soon a curious crowd gathered around the cart.

Danny stopped playing to speak to the dogs. "Come on, Missy! Let's dance for the ladies and gentlemen. You, too, Tuffy!"

He played a waltz tune. The little white dogs stood on their hind legs and danced in time to the music.

As the people pressed close to the cart to see the performance, Mr. Davidson lifted a bottle from the table.

"Who will be the first to have a bottle of this wonderful Duffy's Elixir? It's now offered for the first time ever here in Galena. It cures rheumatism, fever, heart trouble—" Here he coughed so violently that Danny pocketed his harmonica to take over the selling.

11

Danny patted one of the bottles and held it high for the crowd to see. "Who'll buy a bottle? If it doesn't help you in three days we'll refund your money!"

Several of the men standing near him bought a bottle, and so did a few women.

"Let's see your dogs perform again," called a boy from the edge of the crowd.

Danny glanced at his father and saw that he had overcome his cough. He took a gaily painted hoop from the cart. "Now Tuffy, do your stunt!" he commanded the little spitz. He raised the hoop about two feet from the ground and held it steady.

The dog jumped through it, turned, and repeated the performance. Danny raised the hoop higher and higher while the crowd gasped at Tuffy's ability.

Then Mr. Davidson began selling the elixir again.

"Step right up now and get your bottle before my supply is exhausted! Duffy's Elixir, the finest medicine in the world!"

The response was better now and soon the satchel was more than half empty. But so much shouting brought on another fit of coughing for Mr. Davidson.

"If your elixir's so blooming good, why don't you take some for your cough?" called a man from the back of the group.

"Yeah, take some of your own medicine," jeered someone else.

People began to walk away from the cart, some toward the public market and some toward the levee.

Danny's face grew worried as he watched his father. "Don't you think you'd better go to the hotel and rest a bit?"

Mr. Davidson nodded. "I guess so. Blast this cough— I can't see that this out-of-door life is helping me any. The doctor in New York said I'd be much better by the time we were halfway to Colorado. We are almost across Illinois and I'm worse, not better."

He closed the satchel and Danny hoisted it, the table, and the dogs into the cart.

"But Pa, for never selling anything before we've done well, with the elixir, I mean. You rest all after-noon, Pa. I can set up and sell by myself," he said.

His father pulled himself slowly onto the seat of the cart. "I'm afraid that you can't sell alone, Danny. There are too many people in town. They could steal the medicine while you're busy with the show. We'll have to be pushing on from Galena tomorrow."

Danny did not reply but drove the horse carefully down to the next street on the lower level toward the hotel. Then he glanced anxiously again at his father.

"Hadn't we better rest here for a few days, just until you feel stronger, Pa? There's no particular hurry getting to Colorado, is there?"

His father shook his head. "No, only I think I'll do better when we get to the mountains. They say the mountain air is a sure cure. But it's still a long way to Denver."

Danny sighed. "Gee, Pa, I thought we were almost there." He tied the horse to the hitching rail before the hotel and carried the satchel up the steps.

In their narrow little room at the hotel Mr. Davidson lay down on the bed, exhausted from his morning's work. Danny set the satchel, now half empty, on the

floor next to two filled ones. He unleashed Missy and Tuffy.

The little dogs scurried around the room, sniffing and prancing, glad to be free.

Danny sat by his father a little while and then asked, "May I go out and look around the town a bit?"

Mr. Davidson nodded. "I guess so. Couldn't see much when we arrived last night. Don't stay too long." He glanced lovingly at his boy. "This isn't much of a life for you, Son. You should be in school. Your mother wanted you to get an education and have an opportunity to be something better than a variety actor. I promised her that."

"Aw, Pa, I can read, write, and figure a little. What more do you want?"

Mr. Davidson did not answer Danny's question but said, "Oh, well, if the hotel manager's around, ask him to come up here. I want to talk with him."

"Mr. Rowe?" Danny asked. "I'll tell him you want to talk to him, and I'll leave Missy and Tuffy here with you."

Step Right Up!

Mr. Rowe, however, was nowhere in sight so Danny went whistling out of the hotel. He stopped for a moment and looked down toward the river and the levee, uncertain whether to watch the river boats being loaded or to go up the steep steps in front of him to see what lay beyond.

He decided to see the upper part of town first and ran nimbly up the long flight of narrow wooden steps that led to the next level.

Galena was an up-and-down town, built from the levee along the river to the high cliffs above, along the terraced palisades of the Mississippi.

When Danny reached the top steps, he came upon a row of fine brick houses set far back from the street on beautiful green lawns surrounded by high iron fences.

A crowd of men and boys lined one of the fences. They were looking into the yard beyond. Danny hurried toward them to see what the excitement was.

On the lawn behind the fence he saw a company of men drilling and marching. Instead of guns they had pine sticks over their shoulders. They marched, wheeled, advanced at quickstep, halted and saluted their captain.

Although the men were not yet in uniform, Danny was sure it was a volunteer company preparing to fight for the Union.

After the firing on Fort Sumter in April, President Lincoln had called for volunteers. Danny had seen such companies of soldiers all across the country as he and his father made their way westward.

He had listened as his father talked with men in the different hotels. It was wrong, they had said, for South Carolina and the other Southern states to secede from the Union. Yes, Danny was well aware that there was a war going on, a real war.

Sometimes the boy wished he could join one of the volunteer companies, but he couldn't leave Pa.

CHAPTER 2

A Hard Choice

The longer Danny watched the drilling, the more he wanted to join the men. But he finally turned away from the fence, knowing that he could not desert Pa now. If the long trip to Colorado meant Pa would be well again, it was worth it.

Danny made his way down the steps to the levee. Muddy water splashed against the wharf. He watched men loading cargoes of lead for St. Louis and New Orleans. They swung the heavy pigs of lead from hand to hand into the holds of the boats.

He was surprised to see so many steamboats docked along the riverbank. One river boat in particular caught Danny's eye. Gold letters on its side spelled out the name "Neptune." It would be exciting to make a trip on that boat, Danny thought.

Though he had never been on a boat, he could imagine how it would be, with the huge paddle wheel churning through the water, pulling the boat along. It would be much easier than plodding along with a horse and cart over dusty roads.

After watching the river activities for a while, Danny realized that he was hungry. He turned and walked quickly back to the hotel.

Pa didn't seem any better and asked again for Mr. Rowe, the hotel manager. Danny had something to eat in the hotel dining room and carried food up to the room. But his father could not eat. He even agreed to Danny's selling the elixir alone in the afternoon.

Danny took the dogs, the table, and one of the full satchels and set up for business across from the hotel. He saw Mr. Rowe coming along the street and told him his father was anxious to see him.

The boy found it hard indeed to manage the dogs, put on the show, play the harmonica, and sell the

medicine. He sold quite a few bottles in an hour or so and felt quite pleased. But he discovered that several bottles were missing and no money had been collected for them. Then he realized what his father had meant when he said that it would be hard to sell alone. Someone had taken the bottles, but he did not know when or how.

When the crowd faded away Danny packed his properties and carried them back into the hotel. Missy and Tuffy followed at his heels.

Entering the room, he found the hotel manager sitting and talking with Pa.

Mr. Davidson pulled himself up against the head of the bed and asked, "How did you make out, Danny?"

"Not too bad, Pa. I sold quite a bit, but I missed several bottles. Somebody stole them while I was putting on the show."

His father nodded and sighed. "I thought that would happen, Son. Sit down. We have some decisions to make, and I want to tell you what Mr. Rowe here thinks is best."

Danny looked inquiringly from one man to the other, but their faces told him nothing.

Finally his father said, "Danny, I can't make it to Colorado—not now."

Danny nodded. "That's all right, Pa. I think we have enough money to stay here for a few days until you feel better."

His father frowned. "Danny, I—" Here his cough began again.

When he could speak, Mr. Davidson said, "Danny, I want you to take Missy and Tuffy and go on to Colorado alone. I'm sure you'll find Jack Langrishe in Denver. You know when we saw him last winter in New York he promised us places with his troupe in Colorado this summer."

Danny looked at his father and his eyes were troubled. He could not hide his surprise and worry. "You want me to take the cart and leave you here by yourself? Pa, I can't do that!"

His father shook his head. "I don't aim for you to take the cart or the elixir. I want you to go on with

Missy and Tuffy. I'll come with the cart just as soon as I'm able to travel."

"But Pa, isn't it an awful long way to walk?"

The hotel manager leaned forward in his chair. "You won't have to walk, Danny. I've been explaining to your father that you can ride one of the river packets from here to St. Louis. Then you change to a packet for Council Bluffs and go up the Missouri River. From Council Bluffs you catch the stagecoach for Denver."

Tears filled Danny's eyes as he turned to his father. "Why do you want me to go way out there without you? I can't leave you here sick, Pa."

A strange, forced smile crossed his father's face. "That's exactly what I want you to do, Danny. It's important that you go on ahead. I'll come on with the cart as soon as I'm able."

Danny tried another argument. "But Pa, won't it cost a lot?"

Mr. Davidson shook his head. "I have enough money for your fare, Son. Made enough from the medicine to pay for it. As soon as you get to Denver, Jack Langrishe will give you a job and look out for you until I arrive. Remember, he promised us in New York."

Danny nodded. Mr. Langrishe had indeed promised Danny an act with his dogs and his father a part with his theater troupe in Colorado. He and Pa had been friends in the theater ever since Danny could remember.

When Jack Langrishe had returned from Colorado the winter before, he had insisted that Pa quit playing in New York and head for the mountains. There the pure air would surely cure his cough. It was Mr. Langrishe who had persuaded the Davidsons to sell the elixir through the countryside to make expenses for the long trip.

"But Pa," Danny said in a low voice, his lips beginning to tremble.

"Now Danny," his father interrupted. "You're fourteen years old, almost a man. You were fourteen last Saturday, remember? I'll soon catch up with you in Colorado."

"You know," Danny said, "I'd a lot rather join the volunteer company of soldiers here and go to fight for President Lincoln. I saw the men drilling today. Some don't look much older than me."

"If I'd been able, Son, I'd have joined one of those companies we saw back East and taken you with me. But you mustn't think of enlisting. You have to be eighteen anyway before you can join any company."

The hotel manager agreed, "That's true. The war's not for young boys like you, even though you are big and strong. Can't tell how serious it's going to be. I'll go with you to make arrangements for the packet and find out the stage fare from Council Bluffs. I know the 'Neptune' leaves Galena tomorrow."

"Tomorrow?" Danny asked, startled, looking quickly at his father.

"Yes," said Mr. Davidson, "I want you to get packed and under way by tomorrow. It's important."

"But Pa, let's wait a few days and see how you feel. That can't hurt anything, can it?"

Mr. Rowe cleared his throat, glanced at Danny's

father and then said, "Yes, it can. It'll take you several days to get to St. Louis from here. And the Missouri packets don't make trips much after the middle of June. You see, after the spring rains are over the old Missouri River almost dries up and no boat can sail the dry river bed."

"You mean the boats don't run all year?" Danny asked.

The manager nodded. "That's right. They run up and down the Missouri only in the spring and fall. So you have to get to St. Louis in time to get one of those last packets."

Danny sighed and looked at his father. He could think of no other plan to try. He'd just have to hope that his father would soon be on his way to catch up with him.

With Mr. Rowe's help the arrangements for Danny's journey were quickly made. The "Neptune" was the boat that Danny had seen at the levee. It was a fine boat for sure, but Danny wished desperately he were not having to set out alone.

Pa told Danny to pack his few clothes, the dogs' hoops, and his harmonica for the trip. When the next morning came he said, "Now don't worry about me, Son. I'll come as soon as I can."

Somehow Danny managed to say, "Yes, Pa, I know."

"As soon as you find Jack Langrishe, send me a letter telling me you're with him. Letters will be expensive from Denver, but send me one anyway in care of Mr. Rowe here in Galena. If I've left by that time, you'll soon be seeing me in Denver."

"All right, Pa, I'll write," Danny promised.

"Take good care of Missy and Tuffy," his father continued. "Without them you'll have no act for Mr. Langrishe. Don't make friends too easily on the way. Don't trust any of those flashily-dressed, fast-talking fellows. And always keep your money hidden."

"Yes, sir," Danny said quickly. "Good-by, Pa, see you later." He turned away to hide his face, picked up his satchel, tugged at the dogs on their leash, and trying not to show how he felt, hurried out of the hotel. Pa wanted him to do this. He wouldn't fail him.

CHAPTER 3

By Steamboat
and Stagecoach

Danny stood on the upper deck of the side-wheeler "Neptune," watching it chug down the Galena River toward the Mississippi River. Missy and Tuffy strained on the leash by his side, but he paid no attention to them. He was thinking of his father, lying ill back in the hotel room.

Danny could hear the splash of the paddle wheel and feel the throb of the engines under his feet. When the "Neptune" slipped into the broad Mississippi and started downstream, he turned and went to explore the boat with his dogs.

Curious, Danny peered at every part of the "Neptune" from the paddle wheel to the pilot house.

He marveled at the big boilers and the great stack of wood piled on the lower deck. This wood would feed the fires to keep the boilers going. And he was surprised by the luxury of the staterooms and the gaily decorated saloon, the large room where the passengers lounged about and talked.

When he looked into the pilot house high above the decks, the pilot smiled and said, "Come in, lad, and have a look at the river."

Danny stepped inside to see the broad sweep of water that lay ahead.

The pilot glanced at the dogs. "Couple of fine dogs you have. Are you going to St. Louis?"

"Yes, sir. And on to the Colorado Territory."

"Your family too?"

When Danny shook his head, the pilot asked, "By yourself then? You'll be going up the Missouri."

"Yes, I'm alone," Danny explained, "but I'll meet a friend of my father's in Denver."

The pilot smiled. "That's good. I wouldn't like to see you tackle that country by yourself. Let me know if I can help you any. My name's Eli Tompkins."

Danny thanked Mr. Tompkins and felt better at having found someone to talk to.

The boat was not crowded and the few passengers were all somber and rather quiet. Grim-faced men spoke in worried tones about what was going to happen to the country.

At the dining table Danny was surprised to hear some of the men say that they thought the Southern states had a right to secede from the Union. He discovered that most of the speakers were concerned about what the war would do to business, especially to the river trade.

Danny spent a good many hours with Mr. Tompkins, watching the pilot guide the boat expertly past sand bars and snags in the river. Mr. Tompkins pointed out the hill towns, Muscatine and Keokuk, and told Danny to notice how much Quincy looked like a New England town set down on the Illinois shore.

On the morning of the fourth day Mr. Tompkins called, "Come up with me, Danny. I want you to see

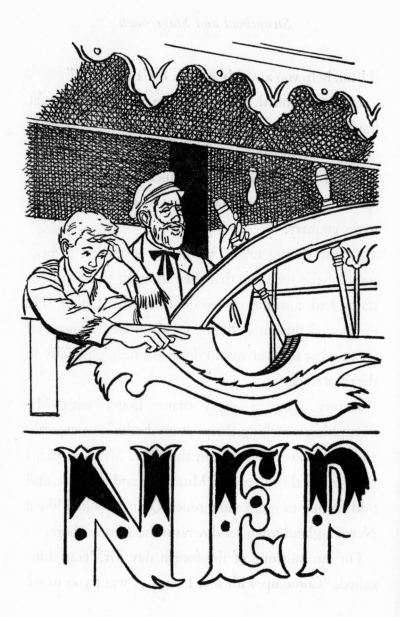

the old Missouri River. After we pass it, we'll soon dock at St. Louis."

"Yes, sir," Danny replied, scrambling up to the pilot house with Missy and Tuffy.

"You get off with the rest of the passengers, but wait for me on the wharf beside the 'Neptune.' As soon as I can, I'll help you find your boat for Council Bluffs," Mr. Tompkins promised.

Then the pilot's whole attention was on keeping the boat in line as they reached the heavy inpour of the Missouri. He was even busier guiding the "Neptune" into the crowded wharf at St. Louis.

Danny had never seen so many boats as lined this wharf. No wonder the pilot had told him to wait on the dock. Danny hadn't the least idea which boat would be heading up the Missouri.

But a little later Mr. Tompkins joined Danny and guided him through the crowd of drays, carts, roust-abouts, and cattle to the stern-wheeler "Chippewa Falls," the Missouri steamboat going to Council Bluffs. Danny stared curiously.

The "Chippewa Falls" was a lighter craft than the "Neptune," drawing only about twelve inches of water.

In another way, too, the "Chippewa Falls" was different from the "Neptune." It was crowded with passengers and freight. The roustabouts were busy loading supplies for the Western outfitting stations. Danny saw barrels of flour, sides of bacon, shovels, axes, and picks being stowed away in the hold.

The stern-wheeler did not travel as fast as the "Neptune" Danny discovered, once the boat was under way. It was lighter and had the disadvantage of going upstream.

The travelers did not seem to mind the slowness, though. They were gay and excited, filled with talk about getting rich in the gold fields of Colorado Territory.

During the long summer evenings the passengers gathered in the saloon to sing and swap stories about finding gold nuggets as large as eggs in Colorado.

Danny found himself listening in wonder to the

tales, hardly knowing what to believe and what to laugh at.

Some of the young men had brought musical instruments with them. When they played their violins, horns, and drums, Danny took out his harmonica and played with them.

As soon as the crowd discovered that Missy and Tuffy were trained dogs, they insisted that Danny put on his act then and there.

Everyone on the boat gathered to watch Missy and Tuffy perform. When the act was over, the crowd cheered uproariously.

The enthusiasm made Danny feel better—he hoped that his act would be as popular in the theater at Denver.

More than a week later, the "Chippewa Falls" reached Council Bluffs. This was the outfitting station for the long journey to Colorado. Here there was a large supply store filled with provisions, stables of horses for the stagecoaches, and a blacksmith and wheelwright shop.

Danny had discovered that eight other passengers aboard the "Chippewa Falls" were planning to take the first stagecoach west for the overland journey. He crowded with them into the waiting coach.

The driver said that the six-hundred-mile trip to Denver would take about eight days. They'd travel night and day, but rest stations would be about twenty-five miles apart. Passengers could get out for meals and to stretch their legs and walk about. At some stations the tired teams would be unhitched and fresh horses would pull the stagecoach on.

From Council Bluffs onward Danny heard no more talk about the war back East. The conversation was about gold for the taking in the Colorado creek beds and getting rich overnight.

Although Danny thought often of his father and wondered if he had started westward with the cart, Danny caught the feeling of excitement the gold-seekers brought with them.

He waved with the rest of the passengers as the stagecoach dashed past long lines of Concord wagons, filled with westward-traveling families carrying their household goods with them. There were mule-drawn freighters, too, and even two-wheeled hand carts pushed by men on foot. Sometimes it seemed to Danny that everyone must be traveling out to Colorado Territory.

After crossing the rolling prairies of eastern Nebraska the coach reached Fort Kearny and the Platte River. From there it followed a well-worn trail along the south side of the shallow, winding river.

Missy and Tuffy behaved well and did not seem to mind their cramped quarters at Danny's feet in the coach. The passengers paid little attention to the dogs as the heavy stage lurched and rocked along the narrow, sandy trail.

When the travelers climbed down at a rest station about seventy miles from Denver a woman cried, "Look! Aren't those the mountains? They look like silver and gold against the sky."

"We won't have any trouble finding gold then," chuckled one of the men.

Stiff and tired as they were from the long trip, the travelers felt better after they saw the mountains. Colorado and riches at last!

Danny did not spend his time thinking about gold. He was eager to find Mr. Langrishe, the theater manager. Perhaps, he hoped, Pa had already started out from Galena.

PART TWO

CENTRAL CITY

★ ★ ★ ★ ★ ★ ★ ★ ★ ★

CHAPTER 4

Ho! for Central City

Disappointment awaited Danny in Denver. Leaving the stagecoach, he immediately went to the hotel to ask for Jack Langrishe.

"Jack Langrishe?" the hotel clerk said. "Why, he's in Central City with his actors. They'll be playing all summer in the gold camps. Nope, you won't see him in Denver for a while."

Luckily for him, Danny had money enough for a ticket to Central City and something left over for a place to sleep and food. Galena seemed a long way behind him, and he longed to hear his father's voice reassuring him that everything would be all right.

The next morning Danny stood in front of the

Overland Stage Office in bustling little Denver. Missy and Tuffy beside him strained at the leash. They sniffed at the weather-beaten plainsmen, the prospectors, the merchants, and the occasional Arapaho Indian who hurried along Larimer Street. The little dogs had behaved well along the whole trip. But today perhaps it was the strange crowd around them or Danny's own feeling of uneasiness that made them skittery.

Missy and Tuffy became so excited when a group of gaudily-dressed Indians passed the stage office that Danny decided to climb into the coach marked Central City. He put his satchel inside and boosted the dogs in through the open door.

As soon as Danny sat down, the dogs settled themselves at his feet and went to sleep. In a few minutes a small, quick-moving young man, not much older than Danny, looked into the coach. "Going to Central City?" he asked.

Danny nodded. "Yes, sir."

The young man, carrying a small bag, hopped into the coach. "I didn't see the stage driver so I didn't know

41

whether to stow my bag away on top or not," he said, dropping it on the floor beside Danny. "Say," he added, "those are fine little dogs."

Missy and Tuffy sat up, sniffed at the stranger, then settled down again.

"My name's Sam Stransky," the young man continued.

"I'm Danny Davidson."

Then the two sat silent until a tall man came up to the coach. He wore a silk hat, leather gloves, and a broadcloth frock coat.

"Going to Central City?" he asked in his turn.

"Yes, sir," replied Sam and Danny.

Then the new passenger saw Missy and Tuffy. He frowned and snorted, "Dogs!" On the opposite seat he edged as far away from the others as he could.

Danny gazed at the man, wondering why the fancy clothes for a stagecoach trip. But he did not have long to puzzle because a dark-haired woman in a blue crinoline gown climbed into the coach. A girl of about twelve or so followed.

The woman and girl settled themselves on the seat beside the well-dressed man. Everything was quiet until Missy rose and sniffed at the lady's skirt.

Evidently the woman had not noticed the dogs sleeping on the floor. But as Missy touched her, the woman gave a scream, rose quickly, and jumped down from the coach. The girl followed, but more slowly.

"Driver!" the woman called, her voice shrill and upset. She looked up at the empty driver's box and then down the street. Turning to her daughter, she said, "Abby, we are not riding to Central City in a coach with dogs. I simply cannot do it!"

By this time Danny and the two men had climbed out of the coach. Doffing his hat, the man in the frock coat said, "Sip Slater at your service, ma'am. Maybe I can help you?" He glared at Missy and Tuffy who strained at the leash as Danny held it. It was plain how much he disliked the dogs. "Ah, here comes the driver."

The woman's words poured out quickly as the driver came up to the group. "I'm Mrs. Edward Mason, sir. My husband is the minister at Central City. Those

43

dogs—I—I will not ride with them." She pointed at Missy and Tuffy, taking care not to move near them.

Danny pulled the dogs toward him. "I'm sorry," he said to the driver. "I've come on a stage all the way from Council Bluffs. Nobody's objected to my dogs before."

The driver looked from the little dogs to the excited woman. "Well now, ma'am," he said slowly, "they look harmless enough, but I'll see what I can do." He turned toward Danny, but Sip Slater interrupted.

"The lady is certainly right. I never heard of allowing dogs in coaches."

The driver scratched his head and then said to Danny, "Boy, maybe you'd better ride up on the deck with them." He gestured toward the roof of the coach. "It gets a bit cold up there after sundown, but I think you'll be all right."

Danny quickly said, "Yes, sir. I don't want to make any trouble."

But as Danny started to boost Tuffy to the deck, Sip Slater gave Missy a sharp, hard kick. She snapped at him in return.

Danny did not know what to say. He hoisted Missy up quickly and climbed to the deck beside the dogs, trying to soothe them. Sam Stransky, who had been standing silent while all this went on, said, "I'll ride up there, too," and climbed up beside Danny.

When everyone was settled, the driver climbed up on his box, picked up the horses' reins, and cried, "All set!" With a crack of his silver-mounted whip they were off down the dusty road.

For a few minutes it was as if the coach were traveling along through a cloud, the dust was so thick. Then Danny and his companion on the deck could see the shining mountains ahead of them as the air cleared.

What beautiful mountains they were! The sun shone on their snow-capped peaks and the long shadows along their slopes seemed to urge the travelers on toward a new, exciting land.

Danny remembered driving through the Appalachian Mountains in the cart with his father. He had thought those were mountains, but they were only hills compared to this majestic range.

"Ho for Central City! Just forty miles away!" the driver shouted. "We'll be there tomorrow."

As the coach creaked slowly upward, then dipped occasionally into cooling forests of yellow pine, the riders on the deck were quiet. Even Missy and Tuffy became used to the rattling, swaying coach and settled down to sleep.

Danny thought about his father, wondering how long it would be before he, too, arrived in Colorado.

After a time Sam Stransky said, "Going out to the gold fields, Danny? You're kind of young to be going alone."

Danny smiled. "Well, yes and no. Are you?"

Sam nodded. "Yes, but not to pan gold. That life's too uncertain for me. I'm going to open a store and sell supplies to miners. I've been in Denver a week trying to get a freight wagon to bring my stock to Central City. It's on its way now."

Danny looked at Sam. "You don't seem old enough to have a store. All the storekeepers I ever saw were kind of old."

Sam Stranksy laughed. "I'm older than I look. Twenty years old, in fact. I've been working for my uncle in New York since I was fifteen. When we heard about this gold rush, he thought it would be a fine place for me to start in business for myself."

Danny smiled. "It sounds like a good idea."

"He shipped some stock out here and lent me money to pay my fare and set up my store. Now I want to find the right location in Central City."

"I'm fourteen," Danny said, "and I'm going to see Mr. Langrishe there to get a job in his theater with my dogs."

"Oh—you're an actor?"

Danny laughed and shook his head. "No, Missy and Tuffy are the actors. My father is too. He played with Mr. Langrishe in New York. But he was too sick to come any further than Illinois when we got there. He sent me on ahead. He'll be coming later."

"Wonder what that fellow sitting in the coach is coming out for," Sam said thoughtfully. "Guess he said his name was Slater."

"I don't know," Danny replied, "but he's made an enemy for sure. Missy isn't going to forget that kick he gave her."

"Maybe we won't see anything more of him—if we're lucky," Sam said.

At this moment the driver called, "Get ready to stop at Golden City. Only stop till we get to Central."

Making a sharp turn and throwing his passengers hard against each other, the driver brought his charging horses to a stop in a tiny settlement. It nestled near the foot of the mountain range.

This station boasted a barn where fresh relays of horses were kept, a tent shelter, and a makeshift restaurant.

The travelers went into the tent shelter to freshen up. When they came out and walked into the restaurant the girl, whose curls had been freshly brushed, lagged behind her mother.

Looking at the dogs and then quickly toward her mother's back, the girl spoke to Danny. "I'm sorry about Mother and your dogs. I think they're nice. But

49

Mother was bitten by a dog and she's been afraid ever since. My father and I would like to have a dog, but of course we can't."

Danny smiled. "I understand. Thanks for telling me. My name is Danny Davidson, and I never thought anyone would mind Missy or Tuffy."

The girl smiled in return. "I'm Abby Mason. We've been visiting in Denver. My father was sent out to the gold fields to preach last year. The Methodists from Illinois sent him."

"I left my father in Galena," Danny said. "I had to come on alone."

The girl thought for a moment. "I don't believe we know anyone in Galena."

Mrs. Mason suddenly noticed that Abby was not beside her. She called hastily, "Abby, come here this minute!"

Abby wasn't to be easily hurried. She said to Danny, "It's fun we both came from Illinois. Hope I'll see you in Central City." Then she skipped to catch up with her mother.

After the passengers had eaten, they climbed back into their places and the coach rattled through the deep canyons westward toward Central City.

As soon as the sun dipped behind the mountain range night came swiftly. There was an uncomfortable chill as darkness hid the mountains.

CHAPTER 5

Danny Finds a Welcome

The next morning the travelers awoke to find themselves riding through a wooded valley closed in by high mountain ridges. The air was dry and fresh, tinged with a pleasant pine smell.

Danny felt cold and stiff from his night on the deck of the stagecoach. But he sniffed the good air eagerly and thought how much better it would make Pa feel, if he were only here.

As the hours passed, the travelers left the wooded valley behind. About noon the coach arrived in a mountain diggings stripped of all its timber. This was Central City.

Danny Finds a Welcome

Danny glanced up toward the sheer mountainside and saw unpainted houses built on stilts in terraced rows. He thought they looked like bird cages hung on hooks jutting out from the side of the mountain.

Not a tree or blade of grass was in sight, but Danny noticed a couple of stone buildings among the rows of frame stores and tents that fronted on one long, narrow street. Young men with shovels, picks, and gravel pans filled the street. Danny decided these were the gold-seekers he had heard so much about.

At the stone Overland Express Office the coach stopped to unload. As the passengers climbed down from the upper deck Sam Stransky said, "See you around, Danny. Good luck with your dog act." Then he walked quickly up the street.

Danny saw Sip Slater swagger into the nearest hotel. A tall man joined Abby Mason and her mother. Abby smiled and waved as she started away with her parents.

Danny brushed his hair back from his forehead, picked up his satchel and the dogs' leash, then walked into the Overland Express Office. "Please, sir," he asked the stationmaster, "do you know where I can find Mr. Langrishe?"

"Langrishe?" the man asked. "Oh, you want the theater man. This time of day you'll probably find him at the People's Theater. Just arrive in Central?"

Danny nodded, "Yes, sir."

"Then I'll show you where to go." The stationmaster walked to the door and pointed up the street. "Just walk that way. You can't miss it."

When Danny reached the long, narrow cabin with the sign "People's Theater," he stopped and looked in at the ticket window in the front wall facing the street. There was no one there so he walked inside and looked around.

The walls of the theater were whitewashed, and the barnlike room was filled with rows of hard benches set on plank flooring. It was dark except for the stage, which was lighted by candle footlights with tin reflectors. A play rehearsal was in progress.

Below the stage, with his back to the benches, stood a tall, lean man wearing a large felt hat. Danny

recognized him immediately. Jack Langrishe at last!

Danny waited at the back of the theater until the final act was finished. Then he hurried down the aisle with Missy and Tuffy, calling, "Mr. Langrishe! Mr. Langrishe!"

The man turned. When Danny had almost reached him, he exclaimed, "Why, Danny Davidson, you're here at last! And with your dogs, too. Where's your father?"

When Danny explained that his father had been too ill in Galena to travel farther Jack Langrishe frowned and a worried expression crossed his face.

"Your father became worse coming out from New York? I could have sworn that the out-of-door life would have helped him."

Danny shrugged and said, "That's what the doctor thought, too. But the last few days Pa could scarcely sell the elixir while I put on the show."

Mr. Langrishe shook his head doubtfully, then said, "Wait a minute." He ran up on the stage calling, "Mike, Mike! Come here."

Danny Finds a Welcome

A short, rather fat man appeared from the wings. "You want me, Jack?"

Mr. Langrishe pushed his old felt hat back on his head and answered, "Yes, come down here and meet Danny Davidson. You remember the boy with the dogs I told you about who was coming out from New York?"

The fat man nodded, peering out over the footlights. "Sure. Where is he?"

"Down here," Mr. Langrishe replied as he walked back where Danny was standing. When Mike reached them, Mr. Langrishe said, "Danny, this is Mike Dougherty, my partner."

Mike shook hands with Danny and glanced at the dogs. "Glad to see you, boy. If your act is all that Jack says we can use you to fill in time between scenes. The audience gets restless while we shift scenery."

Mr. Langrishe put his hand on Danny's shoulder and said, "But Danny, I've been counting on your father to have a part in our cast. When did you say he was coming?"

57

"He didn't say exactly, Mr. Langrishe. But he'll come as soon as he's able to travel. Of course it will take him longer with the cart than it did me on the river and the stagecoach."

Again the worried expression crossed Mr. Langrishe's face but all he said was, "Do you have a place to stay, Danny?"

"No, sir. I haven't looked for one. I was too intent on finding you."

"I'll bet you haven't had anything to eat today either."

"No, sir. Come to think of it, I haven't eaten since we left Golden City."

"Then you'd better come with us to the boarding house now," suggested Mike Dougherty. "It's out on Nevada Street and all the troupe stays there."

Danny hesitated. "Would you like to see Missy and Tuffy perform first on this stage?"

"No, lad," Mr. Langrishe said. "I'm sure that they're as good as when I last saw them in New York. Come on, I know you must be hungry."

"Yes, I am hungry. But Mr. Langrishe, Pa wanted me to send him a letter as soon as I found you. Can I send one from Central City?"

"Oh yes, our stage line connects with the new Pony Express Mail Service at Julesburg. The mail's expensive, though. Five dollars for a letter, but it's fast."

"I don't care how much it costs, Mr. Langrishe. I have the five dollars for a letter."

"If you mail it tonight, your pa should have the letter in ten days at the latest. Write to him this afternoon and we'll leave the letter at the express office as we go to the theater this evening."

Danny smiled with relief. "Yes, sir. I'll write as soon as I have dinner."

Danny walked between the two men as they left the theater and started up Nevada Street.

"The boarding house is farther from the theater but it's cheaper than the hotel and the food's better," Mike explained as he puffed along.

When Danny reached the boarding house he felt suddenly starved.

Mr. Langrishe led Danny into the dining room where a big woman with rosy cheeks was putting the meal on the table.

"Mrs. O'Brien," Mr. Langrishe said, "I've brought you another boarder for our troupe. Meet Danny Davidson."

Mrs. O'Brien glanced at Danny. "How do you do, Danny? Say, you're kind of young to be an actor." Then she caught sight of Missy and Tuffy and looked less friendly. "Dogs! Mr. Langrishe, I can't have dogs in my boarding house," she exclaimed.

The theater manager laughed and said, "Now Mrs. O'Brien, they're the actors, not Danny, so they belong with our troupe, too."

Mrs. O'Brien frowned. "I don't object to dogs for myself." Then turning to Danny, she added, "But I can't have dogs barking and yapping in my house. You see, I have actors and miners here. The actors work half the night and sleep late in the mornings. The miners go out early in the morning and to bed early at night. I can't have dogs barking here."

"Please, ma'am," Danny hurried to explain, "Missy and Tuffy hardly ever bark. I'll keep them on their leash while they're in the house."

"Come on, ma'am," put in Mike in a coaxing voice, "Danny here's too fine a lad to put out in the street because of two harmless little dogs."

Mrs. O'Brien relented. "Well, Danny, if you'll be keeping them quiet and out of the way, we can try it. But mind now, if they disturb people, out you all go!"

"Yes, ma'am, I understand," Danny answered.

"Hurry then and get washed. I'm just ready to ring the dinner bell."

Danny soon met all of the members of the troupe around Mrs. O'Brien's table. Mrs. Langrishe, who was always the leading lady in every play, said she remembered Danny from New York and asked him to sit by her.

As the actors laughed, talked, and ate heartily, Danny began to feel that he had in a way come home. Pa seemed nearer somehow since he had found Mr. Langrishe.

CHAPTER 6

Footlights Flicker

Deafening applause filled Danny's ears when he returned to the stage with Missy and Tuffy for an encore after his first appearance. The noise told the boy he was a success.

From the stomping, whistling, and clapping Danny knew that the theater was filled. But because of the flickering candle footlights he could distinguish faces only in the first two rows.

He was surprised to recognize Sip Slater in the second row. Immediately in front of him sat a young man with the stiffest shock of hair Danny thought he'd ever seen. He clapped and whistled as loudly as any of the men and boys.

As soon as the audience became quiet, Danny played another tune on his harmonica while Missy and Tuffy danced around and around on the stage, their tails wagging.

Back in the stage wings, Mike Dougherty beamed. "Your act is just what we need for the intermission, lad," he said when Danny left the stage. "Saturday is payday for the troupe. Do you have enough money on you until then?"

Danny smiled, "I think so, sir. But it depends on how much Mrs. O'Brien charges for board and room."

"Don't worry about that. We pay that expense for the whole troupe. If you eat any place else in Central, you pay for it. Take good care of Missy and Tuffy, now. Exercise them in the open air every day."

"Oh, I will," Danny said, stooping to pet his dogs.

"After you take care of them, the rest of the day is yours. You can explore the mountain diggings if you like and try panning for gold in the creek beds. Right now you can watch the last act of tonight's play."

Mrs. Langrishe was just passing.

Danny fastened the dogs' leash to a hook where some costumes hung and stood in the wings to see the third act of "Under the Gaslight." He thought Mrs. Langrishe was beautiful, standing in the center of the stage and looking up at her leading man, who was of course Jack Langrishe himself.

The curtain had scarcely fallen on the last act before the man whose stiff shock of hair had caught Danny's attention appeared backstage.

He walked up to Mike Dougherty and put out his hand. "My name's H. M. Teller," he said. "I'm a lawyer from Illinois come out here to establish a law practice. I want to congratulate you on tonight's performance."

Mike smiled broadly and said, "Thank you, sir. I've noticed you several nights in the audience. Glad you like our work."

"I want to see the boy who put on that dog act," Mr. Teller continued. "Where is he?"

Mike called Danny over and presented him to Mr. Teller.

The young lawyer smiled at Danny and said warmly, "I've seen lots of animal acts back East, but your performance tonight was the best ever. You had fine control over your dogs."

Danny glowed at this praise. "Thank you, sir."

"I'll be back next week to see 'She Stoops to Conquer,' and I hope to see your dogs again."

Danny went back to Mrs. O'Brien's boarding house that night happier than he had been for a long time. And next morning, he decided, he'd explore Central City.

The first thing Danny noticed was that Main Street seemed to be the grocery and provision part of town. On Eureka Street there were dry goods stores and on Lawrence there were hardware stores and law offices.

Danny kept Missy and Tuffy on their leash. The streets were filled with scaffolding for new buildings and crowded with men, horses, pack mules, buggies, and water-vending carts.

On one of his first expeditions, Danny came to an old Spanish drag stone mill, an arrastra. He watched

the ox team attached to the mill sweep turning one huge stone on the other to crush the ore between. He noticed how men sifted the crushed ore for the few gleanings of gold.

Walking on through the gully where men were working, Danny came up to a big slanted sluice box. Here thirty or more prospectors were busy. He stopped to see the water rushing down the inside of the box over the sand and gravel shoveled in by the men.

When the water ran out, Danny peered into the big sluice box and saw some little yellow particles along the cleats in the bottom. Gold! He looked on as the men began to scrape the gold particles from the trough.

A few of the men stopped to talk with Danny. They joked with him about finding a fortune. Danny only smiled.

Danny saw the biggest crowd of miners panning gold in a narrow little mountain stream. He learned that this was the easiest and cheapest way to hunt gold, though the reward was not as great as the sluice box or the stone mill produced.

By the end of his first week in Central City Danny had caught gold fever, too. He did not have money to pay for the use of the arrastra or to join the men who paid for the sluice box and the piping of water to it. On some payday soon, he decided, he'd see about buying some tools. Perhaps he'd have some gold to show Pa when he arrived.

PART THREE

GOLD CIRCUIT

CHAPTER 7

Gold Fever

Money in his pocket after his second payday, Danny felt the time had come to try his luck panning for gold. He left Missy and Tuffy in his room at the boarding house and went to buy a gravel pan and shovel.

Passing a newly-erected tent on Main Street Danny heard someone call his name.

"Why, Sam Stransky!" Danny exclaimed.

"See, here's my store right on Main Street," Sam said, pointing to a sign at the door of his tent that read "Stransky's O.K. Store."

Danny grinned and said, "Maybe I can buy a gravel pan and shovel from you."

"Sure, come inside and look around. I've lots of pans

and shovels. Going to do a little prospecting?"

"I'm going to try it," Danny admitted, stepping inside the tent with Sam.

Sam picked up a pan and shovel from a stack in one corner. "You'll find it's hard work, Danny. You don't always find gold either. I've met several fellows who were going back to the States dead broke."

"You have?"

"Yes, sometimes it seems there's as many going home as coming out here. Say, I hear you've been giving a fine performance at the People's."

"Who told you? Have you seen my act?"

"Not yet. I haven't had money for amusements, but if business keeps up I'll catch your act next week. Everybody at Central City House is talking about the boy at the theater who has the little white dogs."

"Are you staying in the hotel?" Danny asked.

Sam nodded. "I have to be close to my business for a while. The Central City House's expensive, though. Say, you remember that flashy fellow, Sip Slater? He's there, too. One day he brags about being sent out here by some Eastern bankers and the next day he says he's an engineer investigating mining claims."

"He does?"

"Yep. But somehow I think he's up to no good. He's too full of fast talk."

"He sure is, and mean, too, or he wouldn't have treated Missy the way he did," Danny added, the scene at the stagecoach door still vivid in his mind. He took the pan and shovel from Sam. "How much do I owe you?"

"In gold dust or nuggets?"

Danny laughed. "Neither, Sam. I haven't panned any gold yet. In plain U.S. money."

Sam scratched his head. "I get five dollars apiece for shovels and pans. But since you might say you're my oldest friend out here I'll make it five dollars for both and throw in a little leather pouch. It's to put your gold dust in when you find some." He took a small pouch from a box and handed it to Danny.

"Thanks, Sam. Money doesn't go far out here," Danny added as he pulled five dollars from his purse.

"No, it doesn't," Sam agreed. "But think what it costs to get food and merchandise out here from the East."

Danny picked up his pan and shovel and said, "Well, see you around, Sam," and walked out of the tent. He set off toward a little creek where a crowd of men were already at work panning.

It was hard to find a place to shovel, but Danny at last took a small space and began to fill his pan with gravel from the creek bed.

He rotated the pan slowly until all the water ran out of the pan. After doing this several times he looked carefully at the wet gravel. Suddenly he saw some tiny yellow flecks.

"Hey, is this gold?" he cried, showing his pan to the man next to him.

The man glanced in the pan and laughed, "Yes, but not enough to mean much. Scrape it out, let it dry, and try again. Seems this creek's about worked out for gold."

"Thanks," Danny said as he scraped the wet gold

flecks onto his handkerchief and spread it carefully to dry. Then he shoveled more gravel into his pan.

Finally he decided that he had worked enough for one day. He showed the small amount of gleanings he had to his neighbor and asked, "How much are these worth, sir?"

The man pushed his hat back and said, "I'm not sure, but maybe you have a dollar's worth of dust. We figure a pinch of gold dust is worth about twenty-five cents. I'd say you have almost four pinches."

A dollar. Danny sighed. He had worked four hours and blistered his hands in the bargain. Now he'd have to make two or three more trips just to pay for his shovel and pan. Panning for gold didn't seem such an easy way to riches.

Danny scraped the gold flecks from his handkerchief into the new pouch Sam had given him, collected his tools, and scrambled up the hill from the creek.

Since he was tired, he took a short cut to town. As he approached Best's Drug Store he was surprised to see someone wave at him. Who could it be?

Coming closer, he saw that it was a girl—Abby Mason from the stagecoach trip!

Abby called out, "Hello, Danny. How are you getting along? I see you've been prospecting."

Danny smiled and told her, "Today was my first time panning for gold and it's hard work."

Abby laughed. "That's what Father says. And not much money in it, unless you use the sluice box or invest some money in the new shaft mine."

Danny nodded, "I think he's right."

Abby looked up the street, then dropped her voice. "Look, Danny, isn't that Mr. Slater? You know—the man who came out from Denver with us." She motioned toward a man crossing the road a little ahead.

Danny, too, looked. "Yes, I believe it is. But he isn't wearing that fancy outfit he wore in the coach. He's in mining clothes and he's carrying a shovel."

"Hm-m-m," said Abby, "I didn't think he'd dirty his hands with a shovel. I don't know why, but I just didn't like him that day in the coach."

"Missy didn't either, because he kicked her," Danny

added, then an idea struck him. "I have my job in the theater, Abby, and Mr. Slater came to see our performance the first night I was there. Seems sort of funny."

But Abby was thinking about Danny and his dogs. "I've heard your act is wonderful."

"Who told you, Abby?"

"Mr. Teller. He comes to our house often. He's a lawyer, you know. He knew my grandparents in Morrison, Illinois, when he practiced law there. And he promised them to look up my mother and father when he came out here."

Danny certainly recalled Mr. Teller. "He comes to the theater every time we have a change in the playbill. Why don't you come, too, Abby?"

Abby looked down and ground a pebble under her foot. Then she smiled at Danny. "My father doesn't approve of theaters. He's the minister out here and I can't come even if it's just to see Missy and Tuffy. But I'd love to—"

Danny interrupted, "Where do you live, Abby?"

She pointed up to one of the little houses clinging to

the mountainside. "Up there, the fifth house in the third row."

"If you'd really like to see Missy and Tuffy perform, maybe I can bring them to your house and give a special show. That is if your mother will let me bring the dogs."

Abby's eyes danced. "Danny, would you? My father would love to see them, too, if they weren't in the theater. I'll get Mother to agree. Be sure to come."

"I will. I'd better get back to Mrs. O'Brien's and see about Missy and Tuffy. I left them in my room."

Abby smiled and called, "Good-by. I'll be watching for you."

CHAPTER 8

A Bad Sign

Two weeks later Danny took Missy and Tuffy up the mountainside to perform for the Masons.

By the time he had climbed up to their house Abby was waiting for him at the front door. She smiled and said, "Hello, Danny. I saw you coming up the path. I thought you'd forgotten us."

Danny smiled back. "No, but I couldn't get a free afternoon."

Then Abby suggested, "Come around to the back of our house. There's more room there for the dogs to perform."

Danny followed Abby to the little backyard just as Reverend Mason came out of the kitchen door.

Abby smiled at her father and said, "Papa, this is Danny Davidson, the boy with the trained dogs that I've been telling you about. He's going to put on their act for me. Don't you want to watch, too?" Then turning to Danny, she said, "This is my father, Reverend Mason."

Danny looked into the stern yet kind face of a man much taller than he. "How do you do, sir? I hope it's all right to bring Missy and Tuffy up here to perform?"

Although his face remained sober, Reverend Mason's eyes twinkled. "Well, we don't hold much with acting or the theater, lad. But I can't see any harm in watching two little dogs up here on the mountainside. Let's see what they can do."

Abby and her father sat down on the back steps while Danny set his hoops down and began to play his harmonica. Missy and Tuffy stood on their hind legs and danced around and around to Danny's music. Then the little dogs rolled over and played dead at Danny's command and jumped through high hoops, just as they did every night at the theater.

Danny was pleased with them because he hadn't been sure how they would behave outside the theater. While he was playing, he noticed Mrs. Mason standing in the doorway, then venturing to sit beside her husband.

When the dogs finished, Abby clapped her hands. "They're wonderful, Danny! Just wonderful! You know, I think that Missy needs a costume. I have a doll dress that I'm sure would fit her, and a flag for Tuffy. Maybe you can teach Tuffy to carry a flag in the crook of his foreleg."

Abby jumped up and dashed into the house to get the dress and the flag.

Reverend Mason said, "A fine performance, lad. Did you train the dogs yourself?"

Danny nodded, "Mostly, sir, but my father helped, too."

"Where is your father?" Mrs. Mason spoke now for the first time.

Danny fastened the dogs to their leash and hooked it over a post in the yard. Then he looked with troubled eyes at Mrs. Mason. "I haven't heard from him since I left Illinois. We were on our way out here when he became too ill to leave Galena. I've been looking for him every day or at least for a letter telling me he would soon be here."

"And your mother?"

Reverend Mason laid his hand on his wife's shoulder. "Now don't ask too many questions," he said.

"I don't mind, sir," Danny replied quickly. "My mother died three years ago. Since then, Pa and I have been getting along the best we could."

"Oh, Danny, I'm so sorry," Mrs. Mason exclaimed, and Danny felt that she really meant it.

The boy began to collect his hoops and the leash. "I must take Missy and Tuffy back to the boarding house now," he explained.

Abby came hurrying out of the house with a little blue crinoline dress and a small Union flag. "Look, Danny," she cried, "Missy would create a stir performing in this dress. And this flag's not too big for Tuffy to carry."

Danny smiled, "Yes, I think that would add to the act. I'll see if I can get Missy to wear the dress and Tuffy to hold the flag."

Just then Mr. Teller came around the house. "I've been knocking at the front door but no one answers. I heard voices, so I came to find you." Noticing Danny and the dogs, he added, "Why, hello, lad. Glad to see you."

"Come in, Mr. Teller," Reverend Mason invited. "Danny's just given us a treat by letting us see Missy and Tuffy perform."

Mr. Teller patted the dogs and said, "Yes, I told Danny he gave a good performance the first night I saw it. I have a feeling that Danny Davidson has more in him, though, than the theater calls for in a dog act." He looked sharply at Danny, taking in the boy's whole manner and appearance.

Danny, in turn, met Mr. Teller's gaze. There was something about Mr. Teller that commanded his attention. He was impressed by the young lawyer. An idea was taking form in his mind. Did he, Danny, really want to stay in the theater and be just an animal trainer and a harmonica player? His mother had always talked about an education.

With a last glance at the dogs, Mr. Teller turned to Reverend Mason and said, "I need some information from you about a man whose case I'm taking."

The two men went into the house and Abby said, "Come on, Danny. I can walk down the mountainside with you. Let me carry your hoops with the dress and the flag."

Danny handed the hoops to her. Even though Abby was younger he was glad to have a chance to talk with someone near his own age.

Together they picked their way down the steep path. When they reached the road leading toward town, Abby faced the other way. "Let's walk out to see where the men are prospecting," she suggested, "over toward that butte. I've never been away from this road before."

Danny hesitated. "It's kind of far, Abby. Do you think your folks will care if you go? It's getting near supper time, too."

Abby tossed her head and said, "Pooh! They won't miss me. Besides, it won't take long. Come on, Danny." She started quickly off.

They scrambled around the mountain beyond the next butte. Danny showed Abby the creek where he had panned for gold and pointed out some staked mining claims.

It was almost supper time and all the men had left the creek bed and the claims for the day. But as they went further, Danny and Abby saw one man busy on a claim. He was not using a pick or shovel. He was busy pulling up stakes and rearranging them.

Abby pulled Danny's arm and whispered, "Look, Danny. That looks like Mr. Slater. Let's see if it is and speak to him."

Danny shook his head at Abby in a warning to keep still. He had a feeling that the man was doing something unusual. He couldn't figure it out.

The man had his back to them. After he had arranged the stakes to his satisfaction, he began sprinkling something over the rocks.

Evidently he did not hear the girl and boy until Abby slipped on a rock and it went tumbling down toward him. He whirled to face the newcomers.

Abby spoke politely, "Hello, Mr. Slater. We thought we recognized you."

The man's face flushed angrily.

"Get out of here, you two!" Slater growled. "Get out!"

Danny and Abby were taken aback by his threatening tone. They stood stock still and stared.

Sip Slater came toward them. "Go on, get out!" he cried, giving Danny a hard shove.

Danny slipped on a jagged rock and fell over the dogs' leash. As he was scrambling to his feet, Missy attacked Slater, biting his left hand.

Frightened, Abby urged. "Come on, let's go!"

Sip Slater examined his bitten hand and began to mutter threats against the dogs. "I'll get even with you for this," he cried. "Get out of here and mind your own business!"

Danny was now on his feet and he and Abby hurried

as quickly as they could past the claims, the creek bed, and back to the main road.

When there seemed a safe distance between them and Slater, Abby asked, "Danny, why do you think he was so angry? We didn't do anything."

Danny shook his head and said, "I haven't any idea. When he pushed me, Missy bit him. She's never bitten anyone before."

"Well, I don't blame Missy," Abby declared. "But I have to get home. It's getting late."

Danny accepted the hoops, dress, and flag from her and said, "Yes, it must be nearly supper time."

But Abby still thought about Slater. "Danny, I wonder what Mr. Slater was doing to that claim. I'd like to tell Papa about him, but I'm afraid to. He wouldn't like it if he knew I had gone that far from the road." Now Abby seemed worried about what she had done.

"I'll tell Mr. Langrishe about it," Danny promised. "Maybe he'll know what was going on. I couldn't see any reason for Slater to be so mad at us."

Abby glanced up the mountainside and Danny said, "Do you want me to walk back up with you?"

"Oh, no, I'll be all right," Abby insisted.

"Then I'll stand here and watch until you reach your door," Danny said.

He waited on the road with Missy and Tuffy until Abby opened her front door. Then he hurried on to Mrs. O'Brien's boarding house. A good many new ideas were filling his head.

CHAPTER 9

On the Gold Circuit

It was the next day before Danny found a chance to tell Mr. Langrishe about Sip Slater.

When he finished, Mr. Langrishe frowned. "I'm not sure, Danny, what Slater was up to. But since you say he was sprinkling something on the rocks, I think maybe he was salting the claim."

"Salting the claim?" Danny asked, not understanding.

"When a man salts a claim, he sprinkles gold dust into the rocks to make the claim appear valuable. After he salts it well, he brings some newcomer out to see it, shows him the flecks of gold in the rocks, and sells the claim to the unsuspecting man. Of course the claim is worthless because it contains no gold except what was salted there."

"But isn't that wrong?" Danny asked.

"Of course, but it's done a lot. If the prospectors catch a man salting a claim, they punish him then and there." Mr. Langrishe pushed his old hat farther back on his head and said thoughtfully, "But, Danny, let's forget you saw Slater."

"Forget, Mr. Langrishe?"

"Yes, if he's working that game the miners will catch him eventually. We're actors, not prospectors, and we want no part in miners' squabbles. Just don't tell anyone else what you saw."

Danny nodded. "I see, Mr. Langrishe, and I won't say anything."

A few days later Mike Dougherty reminded the troupe at the dinner table that they would leave Central City the next day to play the Gold Circuit.

Danny must have missed out on the earlier announcement and he asked Mrs. Langrishe, who was sitting next to him, what the Gold Circuit meant.

Mrs. Langrishe smiled. "It's the circuit made of the mining towns round about, Gregory Point, Black Hawk, Nevadaville, and Missouri Flats. We're adding two new theaters to the circuit this year, Delaware Flats and California Gulch."

Danny was surprised. "I thought all the men came here to see the plays. Do they have crowds on the Gold Circuit?"

Mrs. Langrishe laughed. "Oh, yes, Danny. There are miners scattered all through Colorado Territory and they can't all make it here for the theater. We play the circuit for about two months before we go to Denver for the winter."

"Then we don't come back here?"

Again Mrs. Langrishe laughed. "Oh, my, no! We're at the Denver theater until spring. By the way, Danny, since we're leaving in the morning, will you run to Best's Drug Store and get me some Crisper Coma for my hair? I'm just out and I can't go this afternoon because of rehearsal."

"Yes, ma'am, I'll be glad to go for you."

While he was on his errand, Danny met Mrs. Mason and Abby. He told them he was going with the troupe to play the mining camps for about two months before going to Denver for the winter.

Mrs. Mason looked disappointed. "I'm sorry to hear you're leaving, Danny. I hoped you could come to the school I'm going to teach this year."

"School, ma'am? I'd like that—I haven't had much chance to go to school."

"You mean you can't read or write?" Abby asked.

Danny grinned, "Oh, I can read, write, and figure some. When my father worked in the theater in New York I went to school. But when we traveled, my mother taught me. She used to be a teacher."

Mrs. Mason smiled and said, "She did? Maybe you can go to school in Denver. Meanwhile, would you like to borrow some books and study by yourself?"

"Why, yes, if I could," Danny replied. He'd have plenty of time on his hands and maybe reading would be a good idea.

"I'm sorry you won't be here this winter," Abby put

in. "But Danny, has Missy performed in her new dress yet? Has Tuffy been able to carry the flag?"

Danny laughed. "Not yet, Abby, but I'm training them. At first Missy objected to the blue crinoline, but she's beginning to get used to it. Tuffy carries the flag for a minute or two and then drops it. I'm hoping to have them ready with the new act in a week or so."

"Good! I'd like to see Missy in her dress."

Mrs. Mason smiled at Danny and said, "Come, Abby, we must be going home. Take care of yourself and the little dogs, Danny."

"Thank you, ma'am, I will. And if I may I'll run up and get some books, too."

"Of course," Mrs. Mason answered as she and Abby went on.

The next day the Langrishe troupe with all its stage properties jolted through the mountains in mule-drawn wagons to Black Hawk. The theater there was small but filled the first night with an enthusiastic audience. After a week's stand in Black Hawk the players moved on to the next diggings.

Sometimes during the day Danny tried his luck in the different creek beds with his pan and shovel. Once he found a small gold nugget, but his total gleanings amounted to less than eight dollars. Panning gold, he realized, was a poor way to make a living. Taking out the books he had borrowed from the Masons, he decided maybe his mother had been right. Schooling wouldn't hurt him.

During their last week of the Gold Circuit season Danny noticed a disreputable-looking old man hanging around the stage door in California Gulch. The old fellow seemed to be fascinated with what went on backstage. But for some reason Danny felt uneasy whenever he saw the old man gaping in at the door.

The boy asked Ed Ryan out front who took admissions about the old man. The ticket seller said the fellow was harmless enough and known as Bony Bill, the Squaw Man. He had chosen to live with the Indians back in the mountains. He had been a prospector once but never succeeded. Now he was an outcast, without friends.

As Danny walked to the theater in the dusky twilight on the night of the last performance, he saw Bony Bill standing on a corner talking to a man on horseback.

Danny thought the horseman looked familiar, but he could not see his face. Could it be Sip Slater salting claims here in California Gulch? Well, it was none of his business!

When Danny came nearer, the horseman half turned in his saddle, touched his horse lightly with his spurs, and galloped toward the mountains. Bony Bill shuffled along to the theater.

That night there was an overflow crowd of men and boys. They clapped and stamped and called for the play to begin.

The evening got off to a bad start backstage. The man who played the brass horn in the orchestra was ill, and Mr. Langrishe was in a fit of temper. Everyone seemed on edge.

The play had just begun when Danny approached the open back door with Missy and Tuffy. The dogs

growled when they sniffed Bony Bill, standing in his usual place staring into the wings. Danny silenced them, moved back into the theater, and closed the door.

Later when the boy and his dogs stepped in front of the flickering candle footlights, the audience rose shouting, "Hurrah for Danny Davidson! Hurrah for Missy and Tuffy!"

Danny didn't know whether the dogs were inspired by this reception, but they gave their best performance during the next ten minutes. When Missy appeared in Abby's blue doll dress and Tuffy, carrying his flag, waltzed across the stage, they brought down the house. To satisfy the audience the little dogs repeated this finale three times.

Even after Danny had taken Missy and Tuffy backstage and fastened their leash to the inside of the stage door the audience kept calling for him. He returned to the footlights to take a bow, but this did not satisfy the noisy men. He played several tunes on his harmonica. How proud his father would have been of him!

Finally Mike signaled to stop so the cast could finish

the play. In the wings, all was hustle and bustle as the men packed properties to put in the wagons which tomorrow would carry them to Central City, then on to Denver.

Danny put his hoops and rope in one of the boxes and went to remove Missy's costume and get Tuffy's flag.

The leash was hanging on the door and the flag was lying on the floor, but Missy and Tuffy were not there.

"Missy! Tuffy! Where are you?" Danny called softly, thinking the dogs had squirmed out of the leash and were running around among the big trunks and boxes. But neither of the dogs appeared.

"Have you seen Missy and Tuffy?" he called to a passing stagehand. "I left them fastened to the door while I went back on stage for an encore."

"Haven't seen them," the man replied as he dragged a trunk toward the door. "Maybe they slipped out while I had the door open. Go outside and call them."

Danny ran out and all around the building calling, "Missy! Tuffy, Come here this minute!"

But he was only rewarded by the silence of the night.

CHAPTER 10

A Cruel Surprise

Danny felt sure that the dogs could not be far. He decided to walk around the buildings on Main Street. He even went as far as the big sluice box, thinking they might be underneath or in it. But he found no trace of them.

Once before Missy and Tuffy had slipped from their leash, and Danny did not feel surprised that they had done it now. The noise of the audience had made them nervous, and Missy's blue dress had made her skittish in the finale.

While Danny searched the neighborhood, the play ended and people poured out of the theater. He went inside to find Mr. Langrishe.

"Oh, sir," he cried, "Missy and Tuffy are gone! I can't find them anywhere."

"Gone? Didn't you have them on their leash?"

"Yes, Mr. Langrishe, but they slipped out of it somehow and disappeared while I was playing the harmonica encore."

"They can't be far away, Danny. Did you look in the hotel?"

"Not inside, but I've been up and down Main Street."

Mr. Langrishe gave Danny a friendly thump on the shoulder. "Don't worry. Someone probably let them into the hotel for you. Report at seven in the morning. We're leaving promptly."

At the hotel, however, no one had seen the dogs, so Danny started out again in search of them. For hours he walked through the silent diggings, whistling and calling.

Danny reported back to Mr. Langrishe before seven in the morning. "I haven't found Missy and Tuffy, sir. I've been up all night looking for them."

Mr. Langrishe rubbed his long, thin nose. "You haven't? But I'm sure you will. Suppose you stay here and get some of the men to help you hunt for the dogs today. We have to leave this morning. We open in Denver in just four days."

Danny swallowed hard. "Yes, sir, I know."

"When you find the dogs, report to Central City. If we've gone, you'll find a stagecoach ticket for you at the express office. Come to the Apollo Theater in Denver. Anyone can tell you where it is."

At this moment Mrs. Langrishe appeared, dressed for the trip back to Central City. "What about your dogs, Danny?" she asked.

"I didn't find them, Mrs. Langrishe. But I'm staying here to hunt for them."

She put a kindly hand on Danny's and said, "I'm sure you'll find them, Danny. Then you can join us."

Mike Dougherty had been checking properties in the wagons and rounding up the actors. Now he turned to Danny and reassured him, "You'll find Missy and Tuffy, lad. We'll be expecting you."

"Yes, sir," Danny managed. But his eyes misted as he watched the wagons carry the troupe out of California Gulch.

As soon as the men lounging in the hotel learned of Missy and Tuffy's disappearance they organized a small posse to help Danny search.

Working in pairs, they scrambled over the mountainside through sagebrush and scrub pine and over the neighboring buttes, whistling and calling. They wandered from one gulch to another but found nothing.

At last, late in the afternoon, one of the men called, "I've found one of them."

Danny leaped over rocks and dodged the stunted trees to reach the man who had called out his discovery. There at the man's feet lay Missy, tangled in a frayed rope, her blue dress torn to shreds.

"Oh Missy," Danny cried, kneeling down beside her.

"She's dead, lad," the man said quietly. "I don't know how she got here, but it looks like she got the rope twisted around this tree. Then maybe she fretted and

twisted trying to get loose until she pulled the rope so tight she couldn't breathe and was too tangled to get free."

Danny examined the rope tied around the dog's neck. Then he looked up with tear-filled eyes at the man. "I guess that's what happened. But who put this rope around her neck? And how did she get way out here?"

The man shook his head. "Search me," he said. "You take her back up the hill and we'll go on looking for the other dog."

Danny unwound the rope from the tree and carried Missy carefully up the hill.

The men combed that particular hill and gulch again, but found no trace of Tuffy. They moved on to the next ridge.

When it began to grow dark, the searchers returned to the place where Danny waited with Missy. One of the men said, "There's not much chance of ever finding the other dog. He either ran further away or someone led him with a rope."

Danny looked sadly at Missy lying at his feet. "But I can't go back to Central City without knowing where Tuffy is."

The little posse of men looked at one another and shook their heads. Finally one of them said, "There's not much chance, Danny. But we'll keep our eyes open for Tuffy and let you know if we hear anything about him."

"That's the thing to do, lad," murmured several of the others.

"I'm going to Central City tomorrow," said the man who had found Missy, "and I'll be glad to take you with me."

Danny sighed. "I'll go with you because I have to get word to Mr. Langrishe about this." Then he looked down at Missy. "But let's bury Missy before we go back."

The men dug a shallow grave for Missy, and Danny made a pile of stones to mark the place where she lay. Then he turned away, winking back tears.

Danny spent a restless night at the hotel. Tired as he

was, he still wondered about many things. Was that horseman he saw talking to Bony Bill Sip Slater? And was Sip salting claims here in California Gulch and selling the claims to new prospectors? But Sip's activities should be no concern of his.

Who could have wanted to harm two little dogs? And what of Danny's place in the Langrishe troupe? Danny knew he had no act without Missy and Tuffy. He remembered his father had said that in the hotel room at Galena. And why was there no word from his father?

Suddenly Danny realized that Missy and Tuffy had been more than just pets. They had meant his liveli-hood in Colorado Territory. Mr. Langrishe would have no use for him without them. He hadn't gone to school enough to be prepared for any other kind of work. What would become of him?

CHAPTER 11

What to Do?

As soon as Danny arrived in Central City late the next evening, he went to the express office to see if the Langrishe troupe had left for Denver.

"Yes, they left early this afternoon. Didn't stay in town long," the stationmaster commented. "There's a ticket here for you, but there's no coach going until next week."

"Not until next week!" Danny cried, holding the ticket the man had given him.

The man looked sympathetically at Danny but said, "That's right. The line's operating on its winter schedule now and it runs just one coach a week to

Denver. Most of the miners have gone back to the States for the winter."

Danny turned, walked out to the street, and started toward Mrs. O'Brien's boarding house. Suddenly he changed his mind and headed for Sam Stransky's tent store. He had an idea he wanted to talk to Sam.

But when Danny arrived at the tent, it was empty. Even the sign "Stransky's O.K. Store" was gone. The boy was once again filled with dismay. What had happened to Sam? Was there no one he knew to whom he could talk?

His discouragement must have shown plainly on his face because a passer-by stopped and asked, "What's wrong, boy?"

"Why, Sam Stransky's store—it's closed!"

The stranger smiled. "You haven't been around for a while, have you? Sam has a fine new store over on Eureka Street."

Danny said a quick thank you and hurried off.

Sam was just closing his store for the day when Danny came up. "Why, hello Danny!" he cried. "I heard you didn't come back with the troupe. Did you find Missy and Tuffy?"

"No, Sam. But how did you know they're lost?"

"Gee, most everybody in town must know about them now. Some of the troupe told about it. But they seemed to think you'd find them soon."

Danny bit his lip. "I did find Missy—dead. It looked as if she had strangled herself with rope that somebody tied around her neck."

Sam frowned. "Strangled? Why?" Then he saw how close to breaking down Danny was and changed the subject. "Say, I have a cabin now. The hotel's been expensive and I had a chance to buy this cabin from a prospector who went back to the States. Come home and eat with me. Stay the night, too. It would be a treat to have company."

"You mean it? I'll be glad to come," Danny said, realizing as he spoke how little he had wanted to go to Mrs. O'Brien's when the actors were gone. "Mr. Langrishe left a coach ticket for me to come to Denver, but there's no stage going until next week."

What to Do?

"Come on then," Sam said and linked his arm through Danny's as they started up the street.

Sam's cabin, even for Central City, was a sorry place. It was made of chinked logs and its roof was made of board slabs covered with sheet iron. There were no windows and only a door at one end and a large fireplace at the other.

For furniture Sam had two cots covered with buffalo skins, two three-legged stools, and a rough table.

After a hearty supper of beans, bacon, and coffee, Danny told Sam of his search for Missy and Tuffy. He sighed as he finished and added, "Harmonica players are a dime a dozen, so maybe Mr. Langrishe won't want me."

Sam smiled. "Yes, he will, else he wouldn't have left the ticket for you." He looked at Danny for a few moments and then said, "You've sure grown since you've been out here. About a foot, I reckon. The mountain air and miners' grub agree with you."

"Have I, Sam? I haven't seen anything but my face in a mirror for so long I don't know how I look. But

I need new clothes—these are getting tight."

Sam grinned. "You'd pass for eighteen out here any day."

"I would?" Danny said. "That's good."

As he and Danny had been talking, Sam had been turning a plan over in his mind. Now he said, "Danny, if you'd like to stay in Central, you can work for me this winter. You know I've got the new store. I can't pay much because business in the winter isn't good. But you're welcome to stay and we'll at least eat."

Sam's generous offer took Danny by surprise. But he felt that he had to see Mr. Langrishe. And though he could not bring himself to think about it, he was deeply worried about Pa. He should have been here by now at the latest. Winter was coming. Or he should have sent a letter to Danny. Something was very wrong.

Danny looked gratefully at Sam and said, "Thank you, Sam. If Mr. Langrishe doesn't have a place for me I'll be glad to come back and work for you. I can help you this week anyway."

What to Do?

The next day while Danny was dusting stock in the back of Sam's store he heard a familiar voice say, "Hello, Sam. Where's Danny?"

It was Abby Mason, and she caught sight of Danny before Sam had a chance to answer.

"Danny, Papa just told me about Missy and Tuffy being lost. Tell me about it," she demanded.

"They're gone, Abby," Danny said and told her about his search for Missy and finding her dead.

Tears came to Abby's eyes. "Oh, Danny, how terrible. Who could have done that? What are you going to do now? Can't you come and stay with us?"

Danny smiled at Abby's invitation but answered, "It's kind of you to ask me, but I'm staying with Sam this week. Then I'm going to Denver to see if Mr. Langrishe can use me even if I don't have Missy and Tuffy."

"Oh, Danny—who could be so mean as to cause Missy's death?" Abby demanded.

Danny shook his head. "I wish I knew. And I hated coming back without Tuffy. He might still be alive."

Abby said, "Oh, I hope so, Danny. But I have to go now. Papa stopped to talk with Mr. Teller, and I must get back before he misses me. Come and see us, Danny."

"Thanks, Abby, I will. Please tell your mother I'll bring back her books—maybe she'll let me borrow some more."

"I know she'll be glad to," Abby said quickly. "Bye!"

Later that day Mr. Teller came into the store to talk to Danny. "I heard about the disappearance of your dogs," he explained. "I'm mighty sorry. What are you going to do now?"

"I'm staying with Sam this week," Danny answered. "Then I'm going to Denver to join Mr. Langrishe."

The young lawyer frowned. "I'm afraid you won't have much of an act without the dogs. But I expect that Mr. Langrishe can find something for you to do. Still I wish . . ." But he did not finish the sentence, apparently thinking better of what he had been about to say.

Sam came up and said, "Mr. Langrishe will have a place for Danny or else Danny can help here."

"Well, you have some plans for the present," Mr. Teller said. "But be sure to let me know where you are."

As Sam and Danny walked back to Sam's cabin that evening, Danny seemed downhearted and had little to say. At the end of the week the boy packed his few things to go to Denver.

Danny arrived at the Apollo Theater just in time for the evening performance.

"Hello, Danny," Mr. Langrishe greeted him. "Get ready for your act."

"But Mr. Langrishe, I didn't find Tuffy. And Missy was dead on the mountainside."

"The heck you say! That's bad. Tonight you can play your harmonica between acts and see how the men like it."

When Danny appeared on stage and played his harmonica the men clapped noisily and began yelling, "Bring on your dogs!"

What to Do?

Many of these men had seen Missy and Tuffy perform in the mining camps during the summer when the troupe had been on tour.

Danny hesitated. His lips twisted oddly. He looked into the stage wings toward Mr. Langrishe.

Jack Langrishe strode out on the stage and raised his hand for silence. Then he explained what had happened to Missy and Tuffy.

A growl of surprise and disappointment came from the men at the news. "Have the boy play again then," called voices from the front row.

Danny played several pieces and the men clapped. But it was not the same applause that had always greeted his finale with Missy and Tuffy.

When Danny went to the hotel with the troupe after the last curtain Mr. Langrishe called to him, "Danny, I want to talk with you. Come to my room."

Fear clutched Danny. Was Mr. Langrishe going to say that he did not want Danny any longer? "Yes, sir," he managed to say and followed the tall man up to his room.

Mr. Langrishe threw his old felt hat on the bed and gestured toward a chair. "Sit down, Danny. I'm sorry about Missy and Tuffy, but I have even worse news for you."

Danny looked puzzled. "Bad news, sir?"

Mr. Langrishe sat on the bed and seemed to study his hands. At last he looked up and said, "Danny, I had a letter from the hotel manager in Galena. Your father's not coming out to Colorado Territory."

Suddenly Danny was frightened. "Not coming?"

Mr. Langrishe leaned over and put his hand on the boy's shoulder as if trying to steady him. "Your father died in Galena over two months ago." He picked up a letter from the small table by the bed. "Here's the letter from Mr. Rowe that was waiting for me when I arrived in Denver. Read it."

Danny took the letter. He was a long time reading it because tears blurred the words. Mr. Rowe wrote that Mr. Davidson had not been able to leave the hotel and had grown steadily weaker. He finally died peacefully in his sleep. The manager also wrote that

What to Do?

Mr. Davidson had asked him to sell the horse, cart, and elixir to pay for his stay at the hotel.

Danny finished the letter and looked up at Mr. Langrishe with tear-filled eyes. "What am I to do here, sir?" he asked. "All alone."

Mr. Langrishe patted his shoulder kindly. "You'll stay with us, lad. I'll put you to work. You can help shift scenery and play your harmonica with the orchestra. And here's a letter for you that Mr. Rowe enclosed with mine."

He handed Danny a small, sealed envelope.

Danny tore it open. It was a short note from his father written in a shaky scrawl. It said,

> DEAR DANNY:
> Sorry I can't make it. Mr. Rowe will take care of everything here. Be a good boy and do as Jack Langrishe says.
> > With love,
> > PA

"You can stay in the room next to ours, Danny," Mr. Langrishe said, rising to leave. "Mrs. Langrishe is going to help me with some work downstairs, but we'll talk more about your job tomorrow."

Danny could hardly wait until Mr. Langrishe left the room to throw himself on the bed, sobbing. Pa was never coming. He was gone just as Ma was. Now Danny was really alone in the world.

It hadn't been bad without Pa in the mountain diggings during the summer and fall because each day Danny had hoped to see him coming. But now, even if Mr. Langrishe did say he could stay and work for him, he had nobody. He was alone.

PART FOUR

MARCH, MARCH!

★ ★ ★ ★ ★ ★ ★ ★ ★ ★

CHAPTER 12

Danny in Uniform

During the next few days Jack Langrishe tried to keep Danny so busy that he would not have time to think about the loss of his father and the little dogs. He had the boy help shift scenery, paint some of the stage props, run errands, and play his harmonica with the bass horn and drum orchestra as well as between acts.

As the weeks passed, times became bad in Denver. The Langrishe troupe often played to a half-empty house. Disturbing news of the war back East kept trickling into Denver, and stories of Indians stealing horses not many miles from the settlement made people apprehensive.

Danny in Uniform

As Danny walked along the street with Mike Dougherty one morning he noticed posters on the store fronts calling for volunteers to form a second Colorado regiment.

"Look, Mr. Dougherty!" Danny cried, stopping and pointing to one of the posters. "They want men for a second regiment."

Mike Dougherty took his glasses from his coat pocket, put them on, and peered at the poster. "A lot of men here had better answer that call instead of waiting until spring to hunt for gold," he commented.

"I'd like to enlist, Mr. Dougherty," Danny said. "I wanted to back East when we were in Galena."

Mike Dougherty shook his head and said soberly, "You're too young, Danny. War's a nasty business at best, and it's certainly not for lads like you. Get that idea out of your head."

"But, Mr. Dougherty, I know you and Mr. Langrishe are hard pressed now to pay the troupe because attendance has fallen off so badly. And I'm not earning my keep."

"Bosh, Danny! You're earning your money as well as anyone else."

Danny did not say any more, but many times during the next few days he thought about enlisting.

One afternoon late in January he overheard two miners talking about the war. One said, "Had a letter from home today. My wife wrote they'd had a bloody battle at Stone River around New Year's. Some of our Northern boys were killed and some wounded."

His companion shook his head. "That so? You know, maybe we'd better go home and enlist instead of staying out here waiting for prospecting to begin."

"We can't go home now," the first man answered. "You can't make it back in the winter."

Danny did not hear more, but he resolved to enlist at the first opportunity.

His chance came when Jack Langrishe and Mike Dougherty made a trip to Julesburg in the first week of February. Danny thought of telling Mrs. Langrishe, but he was sure that she, too, would try to talk him out of enlisting.

Danny in Uniform

When Danny walked into the recruiting office, the officer glanced at him, smiled briefly, and said, "I suppose you're here to join the regiment."

Danny smoothed back his unruly hair, stood straight, and answered, "Yes, sir."

The officer pushed a paper across the table. "Just fill this out, your name, address, and next of kin."

Danny took the paper and filled in the places that the officer had indicated. He noticed a space to put his age, but he could not bring himself to write fourteen and he left the space blank.

Next of kin? Why, he didn't have any next of kin. Fearing Mr. Langrishe might pull him out of the army if he discovered his enlistment, Danny put down Sam Stransky's name.

The officer looked quickly at Danny's name and said, "Davidson, you can go with this man to Camp Weld. It just might be you'd be assigned to the First Colorado Regiment, organized last fall. I've been recruiting men for the new Second, but I've had word there are a few vacancies in the First."

"Yes, sir," Danny replied. He was in the army!

The recruiting officer motioned toward another young man who had also just signed up. "Let's see, you're Joe Ward, aren't you? You and Davidson report to Camp Weld immediately. Know where it is?"

Joe Ward nodded. "On the Platte River, about two miles from here."

"That's right. Just follow the wagon trail south," the officer directed. "You'll be outfitted there."

The two boys, feeling excited and awkward at the same time, turned and left the recruiting office together.

Outside, Joe Ward said to Danny, "What did the officer say your name was?"

Danny fell into step beside Joe, who was short and stocky. "I'm Danny Davidson, Joe."

"Does your family know you're enlisting?" Joe asked.

Danny shook his head. "I haven't any family. I'm out here alone. How about you?"

"Same here. I came out from Iowa last year to

prospect for gold. But I've had letters from home telling about the terrible battles so I just decided to enlist."

Danny looked at Joe, but decided against telling him about his father and said, "Me, too."

Joe put his arm through Danny's as they walked along and said, "I guess we'll learn about the army together." There was nothing, apparently, to keep them from setting off for Camp Weld immediately.

As they walked down the road toward the camp, Joe told Danny about the difficulties of mining and Danny talked about visiting the different diggings.

After they had walked almost two miles they saw Camp Weld, its new barracks built around a hollow square. At the gate the boys were challenged by the sentry.

When Danny and Joe explained they were new recruits, a big man—he must have been well over six feet tall—dressed in a Union officer's uniform, came striding across the hollow square toward them.

"New recruits, eh?" he said, his piercing black eyes taking the boys in from head to foot.

"Yes, Major Chivington," answered the sentry.

"Report to the quartermaster for uniforms and arms. You'll be assigned to the infantry in the First Colorado Regiment. We have a few vacancies there."

At the quartermaster's office, the man in charge told the boys he was out of uniforms except for overcoats. The new recruits would have to make out for the present with the clothes they wore. He issued each of them an overcoat, a rifle, and some ammunition.

That afternoon Major Chivington put the infantry companies through their daily drill on the parade ground. Neither Joe nor Danny had ever handled a gun before, but they tried hard to present arms, load, and unload their rifles with the rest of the men.

Most of the soldiers were restless, irked with camp routine and impatient for action. They had been in this camp many weeks. But to Danny and Joe everything was new.

At long last Danny was marching, wheeling, advancing on the double, halting, and saluting just like the men he had seen in Galena so long ago.

Twice Danny and Joe took part in a picket guard stationed every night at the outposts on the routes leading into Denver.

Some soldiers told them the Indians had become more daring, attacking some outlying ranches. The picket guards were necessary to prevent a surprise Indian attack on Denver.

The men also reported that Major Chivington had heard rumors that an army of Texans, part of the Army of the Confederacy, was moving northward through New Mexico to take over all of this Western territory. It was thus that the opportunity for action came sooner than Joe and Danny had dared expect.

Colonel Slough, in command of the regiment, received orders to march his men to the defense of New Mexico. The Texans were indeed on the march to take all of the West for the Confederacy.

In spite of cold and deep snow, the order to march south was given on the twenty-second of February. The main body of the First Colorado Regiment set out from Camp Weld. Joe and Danny marched proudly at the side of men who had been much longer in service than they.

The going was hard. By nightfall the regiment was only six miles from Denver. Colonel Slough and most of his officers returned to Denver to spend the night in comfort. But Major Chivington stayed with his command.

Sitting huddled around a campfire that evening, Joe and Danny felt misgivings about life in the army. Still, there was an air of excitement about the troop movement. This was real drama, not a play on a stage.

Next morning Danny was awakened by Major Chivington's booming voice as he got the troops up and prepared to break camp. The major had been a parson before the war, but he was no soft man, as his soldiers knew.

The regiment made better progress during the next few days as they grew used to the march. Even so, Danny and Joe were often exhausted as they trudged doggedly along with their company, determined to keep up. Snowstorms and freezing rain brought hardships. But the men kept going and the miles lengthened between them and Denver.

Three companies of the First Regiment had been held at another fort and now, about two weeks since the march had begun, the whole regiment was at last reunited just north of the border between Colorado Territory and New Mexico.

"Three cheers for Colonel Slough!" rose from some of the soldiers as the full regiment camped together. But the colonel did no more than tip his cap to the greeting.

"He's not like Major Chivington," Danny observed to Joe. "He'd have something to say."

"Wish we knew how far off the Texans are," Joe said. "They've come up the Rio Grande. Say, how do you suppose it's going to be when there's a real fight?"

"We'll find out soon enough," Danny guessed.

The regiment started up Raton Pass two days later and reached the summit about noon. Progress was halted by the arrival of a Union messenger.

Word traveled like a prairie fire down the line of

marchers. "The Texans are close to Fort Union. Attack is expected hourly. We must march to relieve the fort."

"That must be close to a hundred miles off," the men muttered unbelievingly.

Nevertheless, the men moved faster, and by late afternoon reached the Red River just as the mail coach arrived on its regular run to Fort Union and Santa Fe.

"And then what happens?" Joe said later that evening between bites of food. "The colonel gets in the mail coach and rides off. Just like that!"

"Yeah," Danny said, "leaving Major Chivington in command. If I were an officer you wouldn't catch me riding off in any mail coach while my men marched."

Danny and Joe had hardly finished their meal—the first since daybreak—when Major Chivington had the men falling into line again.

The major sketched in the military situation for his men. Then he paused and said, "All who will make a forced march to save Fort Union, step two paces to the front."

Without hesitation, Danny, Joe, and many others

stepped forward. They were joined by all the rest. The entire regiment had volunteered for the forced march. Not a man hung back.

Major Chivington gave orders that all the baggage and equipment, except for the fire arms and blankets, should be left in charge of the corporal's guard. Then the regiment set out for Fort Union, now eighty rough, mountainous miles away.

With the baggage left behind, the men could take turns riding in the few wagons that the regiment had used to carry equipment. Some of the men rode horseback, but Danny and Joe marched except when they had their turn in a wagon. During that night the regiment covered thirty miles.

Somehow the major rode ahead and secured sides of beef to make a hearty breakfast for his men. Now their line of march followed the base of the mountains, and the men faced a bitterly cold wind. That night there was little comfort because a heavy wind storm sprang up. Some animals fell from exhaustion and died. The marchers made a poor camp without even tents.

By the next afternoon, on March eleventh, the regiment came in sight of Fort Union.

"Look, Joe," Danny said, pointing. "What kind of walls does the fort have?"

"Adobe," Joe replied, squinting to see the fort better. "It's an old fort but the earthworks are new."

Danny didn't like to give away his inexperience, but Joe went on, "You know, the dirt wall and ditch around the fort. Looks like that work has just been done lately."

About dusk, when the nearly exhausted men reached the fort, Colonel Slough came out to greet them. He formed them into a column and marched them into the post, accompanied by bugle and drum. Even Governor Conelly of New Mexico was there and the men heard compliments on their amazing march.

That night Danny fell asleep and dreamed of Texans attacking. But it was only Joe mumbling in his sleep, "March, march, march!"

★ ★ ★ ★ ★ ★ ★ ★ ★ ★

CHAPTER 13

Battle at
Apache Canyon

The First Colorado Regiment stayed at Fort Union for the next ten days. The men recovered from the hardships of their long march. The fort was well stocked and new equipment was issued.

"How do I look?" Danny wanted to know, for the first time fully dressed in uniform.

"Like the greenhorn you are," joked Joe and dodged as Danny made a pretend thrust at him.

Then Danny spoke seriously, "So far we haven't done much for Mr. Lincoln except march and drill. Didn't they tell us the Texans were right here to attack this old fort?"

"I have a hunch," Joe said, "that you'll see the Lone

Star flag before long. One of the officers claims the Texans are just on the other side of this mountain range. He said something about their being near Apache Canyon and Glorieta Pass."

"Those passes through the mountains we can see in the distance?" Danny asked.

Joe nodded. "Colonel Slough's already sent out an advance guard to scout the country and find out where the Confederates are. You'll see, we'll be moving out soon."

Joe was right. On the twenty-second, the colonel started his regiment out toward Santa Fe, about seventy-five miles away. The men followed the Santa Fe Trail wagon road. Four days later, although they did not know it, they were not far from the advancing Texans.

Danny and Joe were in one of the companies under Major Chivington's command. They marched past an old Franciscan mission and Pigeon's Ranch, an inn for travelers.

About a mile and a half beyond Pigeon's Ranch the

men reached the summit of the pass and began the descent into Apache Canyon. It was about one o'clock in the afternoon.

At a sharp turn in the road, charging toward them, came a Union guard. With him was a prisoner, a lieutenant in a Texas artillery uniform.

"We've got 'em cornered this time, boys!" the Union guard shouted. "Give them all the fight you have! Hurrah for the Colorado regiment!"

"Close ranks, advance on the double," came the order from Major Chivington.

The men flung off overcoats, knapsacks, and canteens, preparing for the battle that must surely lie ahead. Danny and Joe grasped their rifles more firmly. They weren't the sharpshooters some of the men were, but they were ready.

As Danny's company rounded a short bend and entered the canyon itself he saw the Texans coming toward them.

There were two short cannon and a company of mounted men. The Lone Star flag streamed overhead.

The Texans halted, took up their position, and opened fire on the advancing Colorado men.

In a moment Major Chivington sized up the situation. He ordered his infantry to take cover on both slopes of the canyon.

Danny scrambled after Joe and the rest of his companions. Just in time, too, for their own cavalry was coming up from behind.

Shells from the enemy's cannon whizzed over Danny's head and grape shot splattered around Joe before they reached the cover of the slope.

All was confusion. Cavalry officers plunged wildly, unable to control their horses or their men. Infantry officers tried to place their companies on the sides of the canyon beyond the range of the Texas artillery.

In a flash Danny knew fear as he had never known it before. He gripped his rifle, prepared to fire when the order was given.

Major Chivington, a pistol in each hand and two under his arms, galloped here and there, shouting for the cavalry to attack.

As soon as the cavalry detachments obeyed his order, Danny, Joe, and the other infantrymen dashed forward from the sides of the slope, firing their rifles as fast as they could.

The road was rough, narrow, and crooked. Danny stumbled and nearly fell but kept going with the rest.

Suddenly the rocky canyon bent abruptly. As the men struggled around this bend they came upon a full company of the enemy stationed on a steep, rocky bluff. Below this company was positioned a set of guns.

Seeing the rebels and their battery, Major Chivington shouted, "Charge!"

The Union cavalry leaped forward, followed again by the infantry.

Danny was terrified now. Musket balls and buckshot zipped past his head, but he kept charging with the other men.

Suddenly Danny heard Joe cry, "Look! The Texans are running away! They're not coming at us any more."

Sure enough, the rebel forces, panicked by the Union

attack, were fleeing the battle in every direction. In their haste they left prisoners behind them along the road.

The Colorado soldiers had won a complete victory for the Union, but not without cost. Several of their men lay dead, some were severely wounded, and several horses were missing.

Half an hour after the order to charge, the enemy had vanished and the firing had ceased. It was now sundown. Not knowing whether enemy reinforcements might come up, Major Chivington called a halt for the day. He had his men gather their dead and wounded and retire to Pigeon's Ranch.

That night the men were tense and alert. They felt sure that Colonel Slough and Major Chivington were planning a bold move for the next day.

Danny, cleaning his rifle, squared his shoulders. Now he knew what it meant to be under fire.

CHAPTER 14

Orders Obeyed

Before dawn Danny's company and some men from other groups—about four hundred in all—were aroused for duty.

With the men standing at attention, Major Chivington explained the mission. "Men," he said, "you have been chosen for a dangerous expedition. We will take the trail south of Apache Canyon, bypass the Confederates' main army, and attack from the rear."

Danny took a sharp breath at this exciting news.

The major continued, "Colonel Slough's men will attack the enemy from the road. When we hear their cannonading in the canyon, we'll attack the Texans from the rear."

The infantry officer gave the order to march. The men stepped briskly forward, Danny and Joe marching shoulder to shoulder.

They had been frightened in their first fierce battle but now they felt seasoned and ready for the Texans.

After the men had marched about eight miles they heard the sound of cannonading. They knew their forces were engaging the main group of Texans. But Chivington's forces were too far from the enemy's rear guard to carry out their part of the attack. Men guessed the fighting must be near Glorieta Pass.

Major Chivington ordered his detachment to quicken its pace as they turned to the right and marched westward. The going was rough. Men had to scramble over jagged rocks and through dense thickets of piñon and cedar.

About one o'clock Danny and the others reached the crest of a mountain ridge. There, about a fifth of a mile below them, lay the Confederate camp.

Dropping down to remain out of sight, the Colorado men studied the layout. The mesa-top camp was ranged about a cluster of adobe buildings. Wagons and draft horses were in the center. A number of soldiers were moving about, some seemed to be standing guard.

Danny heard Major Chivington estimate there were two hundred men in the camp and at least eighty wagons and one cannon. Danny could guess that the wagons were loaded with ammunition, food, and clothing.

The major knew that he had four hundred and thirty men. What he did not know was whether there were additional reserves nearby but out of sight. This was the chance he had to take. He and Colonel Slough had reason to think that the enemy totaled more than a thousand men. How many was the colonel now engaging?

To Danny, Joe, and the other infantrymen, time passed slowly as Major Chivington looked over the camp. Why the wait? Suppose their presence was detected?

At last the major gave the order to attack. The

descent was so steep that the men used straps and ropes to lower each other cautiously downward. At any moment they expected some Texan to see them and sound an alarm.

A fourth of the way down it happened! A man stumbled and dislodged a rock. So did other men. Thundering down the mountain went loose rock.

Suddenly the Texans were aware of their danger. Union forces were swarming down upon them. Men who had been idle a moment before sprang to the cannon.

The Colorado men fired. Texas soldiers had called them the "Pet Lambs of Colorado." They'd show them!

The Texans failed to load their cannon properly. Panic siezed them. Guards and teamsters grabbed the nearest horses and fled up the canyon or off toward Santa Fe. Some men ran on foot toward Glorieta Pass.

"Blow up the supply train!" roared Major Chivington. "Get the horses away first! Spike the six-pounder!"

Orders Obeyed

The major's men sprang to obey. Some led horses away, others prepared to set the supply wagons afire. It would be impossible to save the material for their own forces and they could not risk its being recaptured. There was no choice.

"How do you spike a cannon, Joe?" Danny asked when their squad was detailed to dispose of the six-pounder.

A regular army man answered Danny's question, "Drive a spike into the touch-hole."

"In the breech where the charge is touched off?" Danny asked.

"Sure. Then the cannon can't be fired again."

Two men spiked the Texas six-pounder with a ramrod.

"Now tumble it down the mountain!" cried one.

The squad pushed with all their combined strength, Danny among them. Suddenly the cannon and its carriage went plunging over the cliff.

With his last effort Danny stumbled and pitched forward after the cannon.

He could hear the field piece clattering over the rocks and thought he would surely end up with it at the bottom of the canyon.

Suddenly his fall was broken by a sharp jutting rock. He was bruised and dizzy, but the rock had saved him. He felt a sharp pain and something warm trickled down his right leg. Then he heard the deafening explosion of the supply train and fainted.

The next thing Danny knew one of his squad members was bending over and doing something to his leg, which now throbbed terribly.

"Just a minute, Danny," the man said. "You've had a bad cut. I'm trying to stop the bleeding." The man twisted a piece of cloth around Danny's leg.

"There," he said, "that'll have to do until we get you back to camp." He peered up at the top of the ledge where Joe and another man were looking down. "Throw me a rope, Joe. Get a horse there, too. We have to get Danny out of here."

In a few minutes the men had thrown a stout rope down the mountainside and it had been firmly tied around Danny's waist. Strong hands steadied him.

"Just a minute now, we'll have you back on top," someone called.

The man beside Danny called, "All right, Joe, take it slow and easy so you don't bash him against the rocks."

Danny felt himself being lifted slowly into the air, but his leg hurt so much he drifted into a welcome blackness.

When he came to, Danny was on a horse, supported by the man who had rescued him. His whole right side burned like fire, but he was aware that Joe Ward rode beside him.

"Did we blow up the camp, Joe?"

"Sure did, Danny. Took some prisoners and quite a few horses, too. You're riding one now. All our men are heading back to camp. Don't try to talk though. We'll get you to the doctor soon."

Danny decided later that he had blacked out during most of the trip back to the Union camp. He couldn't remember anything about the trip until he was taken into a hospital tent. There the doctor waited to examine him.

After the examination Danny heard the doctor say, "Where'd this boy come from? He's not old enough to be a soldier. Just a kid, not more than fourteen at most. Hand me a touch of chloroform for him. His leg's cut clean to the bone. He's lost a lot of blood and his right side is rock-burned, too."

Danny tried to say he was almost fifteen, but he was too weak to speak. Then he felt a wet cloying cloth pressed against his nose and mouth.

He thought he was on a cloud when the doctor said, "Just a minute, lad." Or was it Mr. Langrishe talking to him? Or his father? He didn't know.

The next morning Danny awoke to find Major Chivington and Joe Ward standing by his cot. The major smiled and shook his head. "I can't figure how a boy like you got into this man's army. But you did a job, you certainly did."

Danny tried to smile. "Did we destroy the whole camp, sir?" he asked.

The major's heavy, square face broke into a grin. "We sure did. Every last blasted wagon. Took seventeen men prisoner and thirty horses, too."

"That's good. What about the battle in Glorieta?"

"I guess we spiked that, too. It was pretty much of a draw until somebody must have told the Texas colonel we blew up his camp. Late in the afternoon he asked for armistice and withdrew from the pass."

Danny's face flushed with excitement. "I'm glad we helped win," he murmured.

"Get some rest now, lad," the major ordered as he left the hospital tent.

As soon as the officer had gone Joe said, "Danny, I've been waiting to tell you that you've been every inch a man even if you are just fourteen. Here I've been with you every day and I thought you were at least nineteen. I have to go now, but I'll be back soon."

After Danny had been under the watchful eye of the doctor for two weeks Major Chivington came to see him again.

As he stood by Danny's cot with the doctor he said,

"Lad, we're going to give you an honorable discharge and send you home to Denver. You're too young to stay on in this war."

Danny tried to sit up. "Oh, sir, I'll be all right soon. I want to stay with the men."

The major shook his head, "You were a real soldier, Danny, but it's back home for you now. I can't be responsible for young boys in my outfit."

Danny frowned, then said in a low voice, "Sir, I don't have any home. My father and mother are dead."

"No home? Then who's responsible for you?"

"I've been staying with Mr. Langrishe, the theater man. He's been looking out for me. But he went to Julesburg on business and I joined the Colorado Volunteers."

"I see. Well, I'm sending Joe Ward and one of your other squad members back with you to see that you make it safely. Can you sit a horse yet?"

Danny nodded. "I think so."

The doctor did not agree. "He'll have to go in a wagon, Major. His leg's not healed enough to sit a horse. Besides I have two other wounded men going to Denver."

"As you say, Doctor," Major Chivington replied, then turning to Danny, he said, "I think you'll be starting in the morning."

Danny swallowed hard in his disappointment but answered, "Yes, sir." He wondered what Jack Langrishe would say when Danny returned to the theater, unable to work.

PART FIVE

BACK AGAIN

CHAPTER 15

Back to Central City

By the time the soldiers reached Denver with Danny and two other wounded men the Langrishe troupe had left for the spring and summer season in Central City.

The Denver men were delivered to their homes, then Joe and one other man took Danny over the mountains to Central City.

Mrs. O'Brien's boarding house on Nevada Street seemed the best place to go.

"Danny Davidson!" Mrs. O'Brien exclaimed in astonishment. "You've been a soldier, God bless you!" She dispatched a little boy to the People's Theater to get Mr. Langrishe. Danny knew word of his return would be all over town in no time.

Back to Central City

Joe Ward stood awkwardly in Mrs. O'Brien's parlor. Saying good-by to Danny was not easy. "When the war's over," he promised, "I'll be back here prospecting. Take care of yourself, Danny."

When he came in Jack Langrishe was thunderstruck by Danny's unexpected appearance. How pale the boy looked! How thin!

"Danny!" he cried, and he was not acting, "I have hunted all over Denver for you. You just disappeared off the face of the earth. It never occurred to me to ask for you at the recruiting office."

Danny grinned a little self-consciously. "I thought perhaps Mr. Dougherty would guess. He knew I wanted to enlist."

"Son of a gun!" snorted Mr. Langrishe. "He never mentioned that. We finally decided you must have gone back to the States and couldn't say good-by."

"Back East, sir? What could I do there? At least in the army I could make a living."

Then between them, Danny and Joe described what had happened and the two battles. By now everyone

157

was saying that the Confederate threat to the western territories was ended.

"A real hero!" Jack Langrishe said. "But how do you feel now?"

"I'll be fine soon," Danny declared.

Behind him Mrs. O'Brien raised expressive eyebrows as if to say, "That's not likely, poor lad."

Mr. Langrishe frowned and said, "I can't understand why a recruiting officer would sign up a young boy like you. No wonder the Texans called the Volunteers pet lambs—and lived to eat those words."

"He didn't really ask my age. I knew I wasn't earning what you paid me and they needed volunteers. So I just enlisted."

"It's a miracle you weren't killed, toppling that six-pounder over the cliff. Now lie still there and let me think what to do."

Jack Langrishe and Mrs. O'Brien went out in the hall to talk beyond Danny's range of hearing. Joe Ward and the other soldier said one more good-by and left.

Danny must have fallen asleep on the sofa in Mrs. O'Brien's parlor. When he opened his eyes, the shadows in the room were long. He heard voices at the door that sounded familiar. The Masons!

Danny looked around.

Reverend Mason beamed at Danny and took his hand in his. "Danny, lad, we've just heard what a hero you were with the Colorado Volunteers. We're proud of you!"

Abby and Mrs. Mason gathered around Danny, too.

Danny said modestly, "Not so much of a hero or I wouldn't have fallen over the cliff." How good it felt, he thought, to see these friends.

Abby said, "Danny, we have a surprise for . . ."

"Hush, Abby! Not now," her mother interrupted. "This isn't the time."

Reverend Mason was speaking again. "Danny, you need more care than Mrs. O'Brien can give you. It would give us all a lot of pleasure to have you stay with us. I have already stopped to discuss this with Mr. Langrishe and he approves."

"But Mrs. Mason, won't that be too much work?" Danny asked.

"I'm never too busy to take care of a friend, Danny Davidson," Mrs. Mason said with some spirit.

And so it was arranged that Danny should be taken in the troupe's property wagon up the mountainside to the Masons' house. But another caller arrived at Nevada Street before Danny left.

Practically bursting in, Sam Stransky called out, "Danny, how are you?" He stopped abruptly, seeing how pale and thin the boy was.

Danny smiled and extended his hand to Sam. "Fine. Guess I should have taken up your offer and spent the winter with you. How's business?"

"Going great guns now that the prospectors are back. Say, I'm proud of you. I heard how you helped destroy that Texan camp. I haven't got much to offer, Danny, but you know you're welcome to stay with me."

Again Danny felt a warm glow at being in the midst of such good friends. "Why, thank you, Sam. Maybe I can come later. Right now I'm going with the

Masons to stay until I'm strong enough to work. That won't be long."

Sam laughed. "That's a better offer. I'm no cook. But when you're ready, come back and work with me at the O.K. Store. O.K.?"

"I'll do that, Sam. Thanks."

When Danny arrived at the Masons' home that evening he felt as if he had entered another world. The white lace curtains, the horsehair sofa, the shining center table with its oil lamp, the books, and the comfortable chairs were in sharp contrast to the drabness he had known at Mrs. O'Brien's.

The Mason home stirred almost forgotten memories of the home Danny had once had in New York when his mother was alive.

Mrs. Mason bustled around to make Danny comfortable. Abby tried to help, too. The boy found himself enjoying all this attention.

Gradually Danny became aware of something special in the air. It was as if the Masons were sharing a secret among themselves.

Abby was nearly dancing with excitement. "Now, Mother? Can't we tell Danny now about the surprise?"

Since it certainly seemed as if Abby would burst with the secret, her mother said, "Well, ask Papa."

Reverend Mason sat down beside Danny and said, "First, let me tell about my trip."

Danny was really puzzled. "Your trip, sir?"

"Yes, I have a preaching circuit in the various diggings. You might say it's like your Gold Circuit. Last Sunday I held services in California Gulch."

Danny winced as painful memories came back. That was where Missy had died and Tuffy had disappeared.

"I was just ready to come home when an old Indian woman made me understand she wanted me to come. Somebody was sick. I never refuse such a request."

Danny listened intently.

"In a filthy cabin I found a wretched old white man."

"A squaw man—Bony Bill!" Danny exclaimed.

"How did you know?" Reverend Mason asked in surprise.

"He used to hang around the theater when we played in California Gulch," Danny explained.

Abby listened closely.

Reverend Mason continued, "Yes, it was Bony Bill. He was sure he was dying and he wanted to talk with a preacher. Many things were weighing on his conscience. I won't trouble you with all of them. They are not for a boy anyway. But one thing concerned you."

Danny nearly stopped breathing, and the minister continued, "Bony Bill confessed that Sip Slater paid him to steal the little dogs that belonged to the boy in the show at the theater. Slater had wanted the dogs destroyed. They were vicious, he said. Bony Bill took the money, stole the dogs, but couldn't bring himself to kill them."

"So?" Danny asked, hope beginning to rise.

"So Bony Bill planned to take the dogs home and hide them. Maybe keep them for himself. It wasn't too clear. At the edge of town Missy escaped and you know what happened to her. But he got Tuffy to the cabin."

Abby could not wait longer. She ran out of the room and came back with the most starved-looking, neglected dog Danny had ever seen.

"Tuffy!" Danny cried, holding out his arms.

At the sound of his master's voice, Tuffy gave a bark and wagged a matted tail.

Danny threw his arms around the dog, and Tuffy began to lick his hands. Then he nestled at Danny's feet. As long last he was home.

Looking from one member of the Mason family to another, Danny could find no words to express his happiness.

Within two weeks Danny seemed a new boy. Tuffy, now white and brushed, showed few signs of his hard winter. He was so gentle that he even won Mrs. Mason's heart.

The Masons helped Danny celebrate his fifteenth birthday. At the dinner table, Reverend Mason said, "Salesman, actor, musician, traveler, storekeeper, soldier—you've been them all, Danny. But what do you really want to do?"

That is the real question, Danny thought. During these days with the Masons he had been wondering just what he wanted to become. He had done some reading and listened to the Masons talking. Sure, he liked the theater, but he knew he didn't have the necessary talent. He was certainly glad to work for Sam Stransky but he wasn't convinced he wanted to be a storekeeper.

On the evening before Danny moved to Sam's, Mr. Teller, the lawyer, came to call on the Masons.

Shaking hands with Danny, he said, "I've been in Denver doing some legal work and carrying out a mission for Governor Evans. While I was there I had a firsthand report on the Battle of Glorieta Pass. Congratulations on your heroism, lad."

Danny flushed at this praise from a man whom he was coming more and more to admire.

The young lawyer turned toward the Masons and said, "I'm going back East tomorrow." At the surprised expressions that greeted this he quickly added, "to be married."

"Mr. Teller," exclaimed Mrs. Mason. "How nice! But you are returning?"

"Yes, with my bride in July."

Then he looked speculatively at Danny. "I have something in mind for you, young fellow, and I hope that you'll be interested."

"For me?" Danny asked.

"Yes. My law practice is growing in the Territory and I'm going to need help. I need a young man to be my law clerk and pack horse. He'd have to take notes, help prepare my briefs, and carry all my books from one court to another."

Danny listened intently. What was this future that Mr. Teller was offering? Could he measure up?

"It would be hard work, mind you," the lawyer went on. "But if you're interested in becoming a lawyer you'd have a chance to read law in your spare time. You'd get valuable experience in the courtroom, too. After a man reads law for two years and works with a lawyer he can take the bar examinations to practice law."

Danny was too surprised to say a word.

"Well, lad, think abut it," Mr. Teller suggested. "When I come back we'll talk about this again."

Danny finally found his tongue and said earnestly, "Thank you, Mr. Teller, I will."

CHAPTER 16

End of the Road
for Sip

After Danny and Tuffy moved in with Sam, Danny worked in the store and played his harmonica in the theater at night. Tuffy would not perform without Missy but he proved a good watchdog for the boys.

Danny often went to the Masons and sometimes Sam went with him on Sundays. Usually they took Abby on long afternoon walks and then returned with her for supper.

One afternoon they wandered a long way from the center of town to a section of the mountains where new claims were being staked. From the top of a small butte they could see the whole layout.

As they looked down, Abby suddenly pointed

toward the left. "Isn't that Sip Slater? Do you suppose he's out here salting a claim?"

The boys looked in the direction Abby pointed and Danny cried, "It is Sip Slater! Someone should catch him at this."

"Duck down behind these rocks so he won't see us," Sam said dodging behind a big one.

As they huddled behind the rocks, Abby whispered, "He can't get away with this again."

Danny nodded. "I heard men talking the other day. They know someone is salting claims but they've never been able to catch anyone at it."

Sam suggested, "Let's go back to Central and report Slater to the Miners' Grievance Committee."

Abby hesitated. "He might leave. And I think the committee should catch him in the act."

Sam peeked out from behind the rocks. "He's still there. You two run down and tell the men. I'll stay here and keep track of Sip."

"All right," Danny replied. "Come on, Abby."

The two picked their way quietly down the other

side of the butte. When they reached the road, they ran all the way back to the hotel in Central City.

There they found a group of prospectors playing cards. When Danny and Abby reported their news the men growled angrily and threw their cards down.

"Come on, we'll get him," cried one of the men who was a member of the Grievance Committee.

Another man said, "I'll get a rope. We'll hang him."

The men were so angry that Abby became frightened. "Danny," she whispered, "I'm going after Papa. I'm afraid they really will hang Sip. That would be murder."

"I think they're just threatening," Danny said, "Sip Slater is entitled to a trial. He'll either have to pay a fine or get a flogging if he's proved guilty."

"A flogging—how awful!" Abby shivered. "Watch for me, I'll be back with my father." And she dashed off.

Danny led the crowd of angry men toward the butte where he had left Sam stationed.

Halfway up the butte they met Sam who signaled for

quiet. "He'll hear you and get away. He's still busy, Come and see for yourselves."

The men became quiet and climbed carefully to the top of the butte. Sure enough, there was Sip below them, salting a claim.

"Come on," whispered the miner who headed the Grievance Committee.

The men separated, came up from behind, and almost surrounded Sip Slater. Suddenly Sip turned at the sound of a step. His eyes filled with terror and he tried to evade the men and run.

Two miners grabbed him. "So you're the fellow who's made the mischief," one cried.

Sip would not look at them directly. He managed to say, "I don't know what you're talking about. Let me go!"

"Hang him right here," called out one man.

"Sure. Hang him," yelled several others.

"We can't do that," one of the older men put in. "He's entitled to a trial. Let's take him back to town and have a public meeting."

Sip broke away but fell on a sharp rock as he turned to escape. Two of the crowd pushed and cuffed him and Sip fell again. His face was cut and his knee bleeding.

In a few minutes members of the committee calmed the men, took Sip Slater over, and escorted him back to town.

Meanwhile a large crowd had gathered in front of the Central City House. Two men brandished ropes.

Sip Slater's eyes stared and he moaned, "Don't kill me. Please don't kill me."

At this moment Reverend Mason arrived with Abby. "Now men," he said, "let justice prevail. The man's entitled to a trial."

"That's right," replied the man at the head of the Grievance Committee. "We'll hold it right here. Stand back, everyone, and let this man defend himself if he can."

Sip Slater looked into the threatening faces of the men and mumbled, "I wasn't doing anything. Just studying the claims."

There was a howl of ugly laughter from the crowd.

"Plenty of us saw him," cried a man standing in the front row.

"Let's hang him now," called out a hotheaded man.

Reverend Mason stepped forward. "Hanging is not the penalty for salting a claim, is it?" he asked quickly.

"No," replied the head of the committee. "The penalty is fifty dollars fine. If he can't pay it, then he gets ten lashes and banishment from the Territory. Will the men who saw Sip Slater in the act of salting a claim step forward?"

About twenty men stepped out from the crowd.

The man in charge turned to Slater. "You've been proved guilty. Can you pay your fine?"

Sip fumbled as he rummaged through all of his pockets. He came up with twenty-five dollars. "This is all I have in the world," he said, white and trembling.

"Five lashes then," roared a miner from the back row of onlookers.

"Yes, five!" cried several others.

Reverend Mason again stepped forward. "In lieu of

the rest of the fine I say let this man leave the Territory now. If he ever sets foot in any of these diggings again, I will not say a word against hanging him."

"The preacher's right," agreed some of the men. "Let the fellow get going right now."

It was decided that Sip Slater should leave—immediately. The crowd escorted him to the edge of town. Someone gave him a kick to start him along the narrow road to Denver.

Sip stumbled, gained his balance, and ran down the road without looking back.

When he was out of sight, Abby, who had come along with Danny, Sam, and her father, said, "At last we're rid of him. Come on, let's go home."

Later when they were all sitting together at the Masons, Danny looked affectionately at his Central City friends. How good they had been to him and how fortunate he was. He had two jobs in Central City and maybe an opportunity to study law with Mr. Teller. Never again would Danny Davidson feel alone in Colorado Territory.